"I need you."

She'd said those same words to him nine years before. She was a kid then and he ignored her. Now she came to him as a woman with a problem.

He slipped his fingers through hers. "Maura…"

"You know what it took for me to ask you for anything."

He broke eye contact but stayed quiet.

"How hard it was for me to turn to you," she added.

He rubbed his thumb over her knuckles. "I still don't understand any of this."

She recognized a man on the verge of defeat. Saw the signs in his slumped shoulders and the hard lines of his face. "But you're not turning me down."

For a few seconds he just sat there. Didn't say a word. Finally he spoke. "Not this time."

HELENKAY
DIMON

NIGHT
MOVES

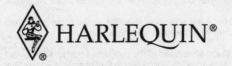

HARLEQUIN®

TORONTO • NEW YORK • LONDON
AMSTERDAM • PARIS • SYDNEY • HAMBURG
STOCKHOLM • ATHENS • TOKYO • MILAN • MADRID
PRAGUE • WARSAW • BUDAPEST • AUCKLAND

Many thanks to Ethan Ellenberg for gently guiding my career in this direction
and to Denise Zaza for giving me this opportunity. My great appreciation also
goes to Shawna Rice for answering all my newbie questions.

To Mica, Wendy, Kassia, Stephanie and Jill—you prove every single day
that women who read and write romance are incredibly smart and insightful.
Sharing the ups and downs of this career with you all is a pleasure.

Thank you to Judy Duarte for saying the right thing at the right time.
Your comments were invaluable.

As always, thank you and big hugs to James for all your love and support.

ISBN-13: 978-0-373-74535-7

NIGHT MOVES

Recycling programs
for this product may
not exist in your area.

www.eHarlequin.com

Printed in U.S.A.

ABOUT THE AUTHOR

Award-winning author HelenKay Dimon spent twelve years in the most unromantic career ever—divorce lawyer. After dedicating all of that effort to helping people terminate relationships, she is thrilled to deal in happy endings and write romance novels for a living. Now her days are filled with gardening, writing, reading and spending time with her family in and around San Diego. HelenKay loves hearing from readers, so stop by her Web site at www.helenkaydimon.com and say hello.

Books by HelenKay Dimon

HARLEQUIN INTRIGUE
1196—UNDER THE GUN
1214—NIGHT MOVES

CAST OF CHARACTERS

Liam Anderson—Finding out his best friend's little sister is dead is a huge shock. Discovering her very much alive and hiding in his house leads him on a wild chase to clear her name and earn her forgiveness for the past.

Dr. Maura Lindsey—The brilliant scientist might not be good with people but she knows falsified research results when she sees them. When the discovery is followed by an explosion that nearly kills her, she turns to the man who once broke her heart.

Dr. Langdon Hammer—The reclusive doctor disappears just as he makes the greatest find of his career. Was he kidnapped, killed or is something even worse going on?

Rex Smithfield—A businessman who made his name and fortune bringing pharmaceuticals to the public. Now he wants Dr. Hammer's research and is willing to do almost anything to get it.

Dan Lindsey—Maura's brother and Liam's best friend who, even while lost in grief, refuses to believe his sister is a criminal.

Detective Rick Spanner—The detective assigned to track down Maura when she goes missing. When Liam, a former police officer, insists he hasn't seen Maura, Spanner knows he's stumbled into a bigger story than he imagined.

Patricia Hammer—Dr. Hammer's new young wife. She enjoys her husband's prestige and all the benefits it brings. And she isn't willing to give up her newfound social position without a fight.

Chapter One

"Tell me how much she knows."

"She is a very able student." Dr. Langdon Hammer felt a surge of pride at having picked his assistant. Maura Lindsey possessed multiple degrees and a significant amount of research experience. Not just any lab could secure the services of such a dedicated and knowledgeable young doctor.

Of course, the very reasons that made her ideal as a professional also made her a problem now. Being brilliant would be her downfall.

"I'm talking about professionally, Hammer."

"So am I. She works with me every day. Just work." Dr. Hammer didn't bother to look up from the computer keyboard. He couldn't type if he couldn't see the letters, and he had to move fast. The man standing in front of him didn't like having his time wasted.

Just thinking about the man's plans made Dr. Hammer's fingers trip over the keys and accidentally erase an entire column of data. This was why he had an assistant. Entering information and other menial tasks fell to her.

"Tell me about her access to your work. How much does she see?" the other man asked.

Dr. Hammer's hand hesitated over the delete key. "All of it."

"Does she understand the ramifications of your findings?"

"Of course." As if he would hire someone incapable of grasping a world-changing scientific breakthrough. Stupid people annoyed him.

The other man paced the small space across from Dr. Hammer, the only section of the office not blocked by stacks of books and papers. "Then she's the logical choice for this."

Dr. Hammer tried one last time to argue for her. "She is invaluable to my research."

"Everyone is replaceable."

Dr. Hammer pushed back in his chair and focused solely on the conversation. The disturbing turn had his full attention now. "Not everyone."

"There are others with the same level of expertise as you."

"Hardly."

"With enough assistance, they can reach your level."

"That would take years, possibly decades, and even then it's doubtful. On the other hand, there is no question about my success. I have achieved it."

"Which is why we came to you." The man traced his finger over the top of the crystal award sitting on the edge of Dr. Hammer's desk. "But you would be wise to remember the extent of my resources. The reach of my power."

Dr. Hammer swallowed back the lump of fear that had been forming since the other man walked into the office. "I am."

"Then we understand each other."

"Yes."

The man's twisted grin resembled that of a pouncing animal. "Dr. Lindsey will continue to help you. She just needs to be dead to do it."

MAURA LINDSEY READ OVER the paragraph a second time. She didn't need her two doctorate degrees and a genius-level IQ to recognize something was very wrong at the Systems Institute, the government lab where she worked.

Since the task of inputting information, complying with regulations and keeping track of the paperwork fell to her, there was no way this amounted to a simple misunderstanding. Altered data and wrong conclusions. It was all right there in front of her. No matter how many times she blinked, the words in the file didn't change. Her boss, Dr. Langdon Hammer, had prepared a false interim report on their organ transplant research for the National Institutes of Health. The same report he hid from her.

He had always been eccentric. Grumpy and brilliant, private and utterly focused on his research to the point of distraction over everything except, maybe, his new wife. Married or not, he definitely was not a people person and lately he added secretive to his list of unattractive attributes.

Maura ignored the sharp change in his temperament at first. She understood the pressure of working long lonely hours in a sterile lab in the rush for groundbreaking scientific developments. But she didn't understand the lies.

She stood in the center of Dr. Hammer's office with two sets of notes in her hands. The real ones and the ones her boss compiled for his progress report. His *fake* progress report.

She only saw one solution—take the documents and review them somewhere else. It was a violation of her employment, and she hated to take the risk, but if Dr. Hammer saw her pawing through his papers or suspected she had questions, she might never get the answers she needed. She'd go home, spread everything out across her dining-room table and study the data. Maybe there was a reasonable explanation. If not, she'd get someone high up in NIH to listen to her concerns.

Heavy footsteps fell in the hallway, breaking into her mental plotting. The unknown visitor didn't stop or question the light being on in Dr. Hammer's office. The quick pace suggested running and no one ran in the Institute. Other than a few offices—most of which were empty—and a small area for administrative and computer work, the main floor consisted only of lab space. And only two people worked there. Dr. Hammer insisted on keeping the people with access to his findings to a minimum.

The floor above housed another lab engaged in unrelated government research on top-secret projects, but it was ten o'clock on Saturday night. Only people without a life were in the building now, and that meant she was alone except for the security guard at the front door.

"Tom?" When he didn't answer, Maura tried again. "Hello?"

She gathered up all the files on Dr. Hammer's desk and shoved them under her arm. She wanted to download everything from her boss's computer onto a drive, but the usual password didn't work. Seemed the absent-minded scientist had instituted some new security protocols that day without telling her. Since the man could barely order lunch without someone dialing the phone for him, she feared what was happening might involve Dr. Hammer using outside resources, which violated just about every clause of his confidentiality agreement and employment contract with the government.

But she'd figure that out later. Right now, she had to move.

Being as quiet as possible, she peeked out the office doorway, then slid into the hallway. If someone who shouldn't be running around was out there, she sure didn't want to meet up with him. Getting caught with stolen documents was not the way for her to keep her job, and she had worked too hard to get this assignment to lose it now.

Being attacked by a crazed burglar was not on her agenda, either.

She listened for any noise. She expected the natural sounds of the building to echo back to her. A creak here or there. The hum of lights and machines. An occasional ring of a phone. She heard nothing, and in this case, that was a very bad thing. The deadly stillness set off a whirl of panic in her stomach.

She took a few steps and glanced down to the far end of the hallway. All the doors along the way to the private offices remained closed. The steel entry to the lobby area looked to be locked up tight. The lights on the alarm panel next to it flashed green, just like they were supposed to do.

That direction checked out. So, she looked over her shoulder, back the other way to the matching panel at the opposite end of the corridor. It was the one closest to her and it led to the lab, and it was deadly dark.

Problem found.

No whistles or screaming bells. The fingerprint scanner was in place but not lit up as usual. The fact that the door stood wide open qualified as the biggest problem of the moment. She couldn't see inside, but didn't have to. They kept the door locked. Always.

The potential danger of the situation hit her with a clarity that threatened to knock her over, even as her brain struggled to analyze what she was seeing. Not trusting her mind to sort it all out fast enough, she fumbled in her lab-coat pocket, searching for her cell phone to call the police. It wasn't there. As usual, she'd put it down somewhere and lost track of it. Her brother insisted that habit would get her in trouble one day. She feared that day had come.

She was stuck away from the phones with nothing more than a stack of papers in her hands for protection. Defenseless and alone, the combination sent her mind spinning. Her usual calm abandoned her in favor of grinding panic. Every inch of her shook with the need to escape and find help.

She felt her way along the wall as she inched down the hallway toward the lobby and freedom. Her breath pounded in her chest, scratching her throat raw. A squeak of shoes against the tile floor stopped her. She bit down on her tongue to keep from shouting for Tom. He would have answered her before if he could have. He wouldn't play around in the lab.

No, this was someone else—stalking, hiding, waiting for her.

Forget quiet. She needed speed. She ran back into Dr. Hammer's office and headed for the phone. Before she could reach for the receiver, a deafening whoosh thundered up the hall, shattering glass in its wake. As she struggled to see what was happening, a huge boom rattled the building. The ground beneath her shook with enough force to buckle her knees and send vibrations up her legs.

A second explosion sent her body flying into Dr. Hammer's huge mahogany desk. Her middle smacked into the edge, stealing her breath and scattering papers around her feet. Her vision swirled at the edges as she fell to the floor. For a second, she closed her eyes, hoping to open them again and find out this was nothing more than a nightmare.

A harsh banging brought her back to the present. Smoke filled the hallway and heat enveloped her. She choked on the foul air as she looked around. She tried to process the events of the last few minutes but her mind refused to function.

One thing was clear. She had to get out of there. Crackling sounded all around her as the building heaved and groaned. If she didn't find fresh air and get out soon, she'd be crushed or burned alive. She refused to be a victim of either option.

On her hands and knees, she crawled across shards of glass and ignored the edges as they bit into her skin. She drew up a mental floor plan of the office and aimed for where the window should be. She'd crash through it if she had to. Anything to get outside and away from the building before it imploded.

With her mouth tucked into the sleeve of her coat, she lifted to her feet in a bent-over crouch. From this position she could see what remained of the office space. Nothing separated it from the hall now. The wall between Dr. Hammer's office and hers had collapsed, leaving a blown-out opening. Fire danced in every inch of her room as bright orange flames raced up her walls, swallowing her framed degrees and bookshelves in one hot gulp.

If she had been where she was supposed to be, she'd be dead. Snooping had saved her.

Ceiling tiles fell from above her head, barely missing her. The walls were buckling. The thundering mix of fire and falling debris filled her ears. The taste of soot lingered on her tongue. There would be nothing left soon, including her, if she didn't jump through the window. The glass had shattered leaving ragged edges. Using her elbow, she cleared a path and wiggled out the small opening. A final pop propelled her outside, throwing her through the air until she landed hard on her right side on the grassy area outside.

Pain crushed in on her from every angle as she rolled as far away from the burning structure as possible. She hurt everywhere. Her mind reeled and fingers burned. When she looked down, she saw the death grip she had on some of those files. Through all the shock and the explosions, she had held on. The realization sent a wave of relief through her. She didn't know where the papers fit together with the explosions, but she sensed on some level they did.

She dropped her head back and tried to gather the energy to get up. Smoke spiraled into the dark sky. Alarms hadn't sounded, but she held out hope someone had heard the crashing booms that even now continued to sound, or saw the flames licking against the cloudless night.

Their building sat at the end of a long private drive in McLean, Virginia. The secluded setting ensured security, or that was the theory. Now the isolation worked against her, guaranteeing that precious data she needed would be lost before the fire department got word and came screaming to the scene.

When she lifted her head again and glanced around, she could make out the outline of a large SUV near the entrance to the building. It was a car that hadn't been there when she checked in earlier. A second later, three people piled out of the front door in a rush. The bright lights of the outside parking area let her see what was happening. She recognized the straight-backed and serious steps of Dr. Hammer. He wasn't injured. If anything, he maintained his usual even pace while the men around him tried to hustle him.

Before she could call out his name, one of

the other men opened the back door of the vehicle and signaled for Dr. Hammer to get in. With one last long look at the Institute, he slipped in and closed the door. The SUV took off, leaving her alone and the disaster behind.

Maura tried to put the bits she knew together in a reasonable story, but the last hour didn't make any sense. Dr. Hammer's precious work was vanishing in front of him and he didn't show any more concern than he did on a normal day when he left the office. More important, he didn't seem to notice her car was in the parking lot while the building was on fire. Either he didn't care that she could be injured or dead or worse, he wanted her to be.

She couldn't figure out why, but she knew everything had gone wrong. This was more than a problem with the interim report. This went deeper. The fire and the false data were connected somehow. Had to be.

Anxiety flooded through her, making every cell in her body quake and tremble. She didn't know who to trust or where to go.

No, that wasn't true. She knew exactly

where to go and who could help her untangle the mess.

Ignoring the pain in her shoulder and aches everywhere else, she rolled to her knees. She had to get up and go to Liam. She'd run away from him for years, but now she needed him. Liam would know what to do.

The plan set, she shot up too fast. Dizziness slammed through her the second her feet hit the ground. The move sent her back to her knees. She tried to gulp in air, but it was too late. The shot of adrenaline that guided her through the last few minutes had worn off, leaving behind a blinding headache and exhaustion she couldn't shake.

When her elbows gave out, she fell back to the ground and stayed there, staring up into the black night. Yes, Liam would help. She repeated that mantra until she convinced herself it was true. Now she had to convince him.

Chapter Two

Liam Anderson had been to more memorial services than he could count. A devastated family, shocked loved ones. He knew the drill and always steeled himself against getting sucked into the sad aftermath of someone else's violent end. But the last twenty hours had been different.

This wasn't about paying his respects to a victim's family in a case. This was about getting through those initial horrible hours after the bad news came. This was for Maura, his best friend's sister.

Twenty-four and dead. It didn't seem possible. Sitting there and watching Dan descend into madness made it real for Liam. His friend had spent almost every hour in a drunken haze since getting the unbelievable news. Dan only sobered up this afternoon when the police showed up a second time, changed tactics and started asking questions about Maura's background. They danced around the accusations but it was clear they believed she had something to do with the explosion.

Liam provided support and an ear. Even got pissed off on Maura's behalf at the accusations. Keeping Dan from crawling all over the cops proved harder. Liam left only after Dan had settled down, but planned to return to Dan's house after a shower and change of clothes. Keeping Dan sane was the only way Liam knew to beat back his own feelings.

Maura had run from him and now she was gone forever. He would never have a chance to apologize and make things right for what happened nine years earlier. Never get to know the woman she'd become. He'd be stuck with only the memories of a brokenhearted girl.

He shook his head as he slammed his car door. What a waste.

Within two steps, Liam realized something was off at his house. He was a security expert, after all. It was his business to notice things, to sense danger, analyze it and diffuse it. His gaze swept over the front lawn and up the porch to his door. He visually checked his alarm and the other traps he set around the entrance every time he went out, but nothing seemed obviously out of place there.

Still, the prickling sensation didn't ease. He'd learned long ago to pay attention when a sharp pain whacked him between the shoulder blades. He failed to listen exactly one time in his professional life and had the scar on his leg to prove it. He intended to heed the warning this time.

Unfortunately, his weapons all sat securely inside. He'd never imagined he'd need a gun today. Violence should take one day off.

He scanned the area again, looking for any change no matter how small. The gate to the side yard on the right of his place caught his attention. Every time he closed it, he pulled it tight enough for the gate to swing inside the yard slightly. The gate hung even with the fence now. That meant someone had used the walkway to get to his backyard, outside of the view of the street.

Smart, but not smart enough.

The fact the alarm had not been tripped made him think the burglar never made it inside the house. Liam hoped like hell the guy was still around. It would feel good to pound someone right about now, to work out all of his aggression and anger at Maura's loss.

Liam knew he had surprise on his side. His dark jeans would provide some camouflage but the white oxford would give his position away. The important thing was he had the freedom of movement he needed to get the jump on whoever wanted inside his house.

If he disengaged the alarm it would beep, so he decided to go with the soundless option: circle around the left side and hunt this guy down from the outside. No need to dissect the plan. He got moving.

He lifted the latch and stalked along the side of the house, careful not to tip off anyone to his location. His feet fell quiet against the soft grass as he inched along the red-brick wall. When he reached the corner, he peeked around to the patio and saw a figure slumped in one of his deck chairs. All he could make out were slats of wood and a mop of brown hair.

He pounced, hitting the deck at a dead run. At the last minute, his unwanted visitor turned around. Recognition washed through him, but it was too late for Liam to change his path. He crashed into the chair, sending them both careening toward the hardwood floor. Liam managed to twist his body and shoulder most of the impact, but they both went down with a *humph*.

He groaned as his muscles recovered from the jolt. "Maura?"

She sprawled on top of him not moving.

"Hey!" He held on to her and struggled to sit up despite his awkward position, and about a hundred-thirty pounds of extra weight piled on top of him. "Are you okay?"

She mumbled something that sounded like words but didn't make much sense.

Her long hair hung down in her face, but at least she was alive. "What are you doing back here? Why aren't you at Dan's house? The police think—"

Her chest rose and fell on heavy breaths as she stared at him. "Do you welcome everyone that way?"

Liam shook his head, trying to make sense of what he was seeing. Who he was seeing. "What the hell is going on?"

"That tackle wasn't as bad as the fire, but close."

"You're supposed to be dead." Not the

brightest conversation starter ever, but he figured it got the job done.

Confusion cleared from her eyes. "Well, I'm not."

He gave her a little squeeze then shifted her to the side and off his injured leg as gently as possible. He took a long look at her. He rarely saw her despite his relationship with Dan. When he did, Liam was struck by a beautiful woman with a round face and big chocolate-brown eyes. Curvy, with shiny hair and wide smile.

Now she had cuts on her hands and face. A bruise colored her cheek. Her clothes hung loose as if she showered and threw on someone else's tee and pants.

"Let's try my first question again. Are you okay?" he asked.

"I was, until about three seconds ago when you pummeled me."

"Thought you were a burglar."

She brushed her hands up and down her arms. "You have an interesting way of protecting your property."

She had no idea what he was capable of. "I don't understand what's going on. Dan thinks you're dead. Everyone does."

"Can we go inside?"

It was a cool April day and she was dressed for summer, but the weather was just about the last thing on his mind. "Explain first."

"Inside." She glanced around and then leaned in to whisper. "Please."

No way could he fight that scared look on her face. He struggled to his feet and held a hand down to help her up. Her fingers felt like ice against his skin. "You could have gone in."

"You have enough security here for a small city." She nodded toward the alarm panel. "Without the code, I wasn't about to risk it. I didn't want the police to come."

"Why?"

She dropped his hand. "I'll explain once we get inside. Promise."

The fence and tall trees gave them privacy, but the way she chewed on her lower lip suggested she didn't feel all that safe. Paranoid and hunted—words he never would have used to describe her before. But they worked now. She'd aged before his eyes.

It was official. He had no idea what was going on. That wasn't exactly a new sensation where Maura was concerned, but this wasn't about her fancy job and impressive book smarts. This was a common-sense matter of talking to the police. Seemed simple to him.

"Let's go." When he reached over to guide her to the door with a hand at her back, she flinched. The reaction surprised him. Ticked him off, too. "Are you afraid of me now?"

The taunt came more from habit than anything else. She had been avoiding him for so long that he expected her to do nothing else.

Her chin lifted. "Of course not."

He noticed she cradled her right arm and immediately regretted the verbal battle. He knew that protective maneuver. It probably meant injury. When he asked all of the other questions swimming in his mind, he'd ask that one, too. But for now, he wanted her talking. The faster they did that, the faster he could call Dan and save his friend's liver from the pickling it had been subjected to for the last few hours.

"Where have you been?" Liam asked.

"Hiding."

After a quick set of punches on the keypad, Liam opened the door and motioned for her to step inside. He expected her to walk through the kitchen to his family room and curl up on the couch. Instead, she hunkered down on the bar stool and stared at his fridge.

He tried to assess her mood and failed. "Are you hurt?"

She rubbed her arm. Probably didn't even realize she did it. "Sore, but otherwise okay."

"How about hungry?"

"No."

He roamed around his kitchen looking for a way to keep his hands busy. "Thirsty?"

"Just some water, please."

He grabbed a bottle and twisted off the cap before setting it in front of her. "Yeah, I hear dying can be dehydrating."

She treated him to a slight smile then. "That's what they say."

His patience picked that moment to expire. He went from being supportive to being frustrated. The latter emotion he knew well in conjunction with Maura. "Look, I'm all for small talk but why don't we skip to the part where you explain what's going on?"

She took a long drink, drawing out the silence, then picked at the bottle's label. "There was an explosion."

"I know that much."

She frowned at him. "Let me finish."

With the shock gone, all he had left was the churning anger in his gut. "Your brother is sitting at his house drinking himself into a black oblivion while he mourns your death. So, forgive me if I'm confused why you're here and not there. Why you're anywhere, for that matter."

Pain flashed across her face. "Dan."

"Yeah, Maura. Dan." Liam leaned down on his elbows until they were face-to-face. "You're not the type who would let her brother worry for no reason. What is this?"

"I was in the building when it exploded." She lifted her hand to stop him when he tried to butt in. "I...saw something."

"What?"

"Dr. Hammer."

Yeah, him. "I'm sorry about that, Maura."

All emotion left her face. "For what?"

"You wanted to work for someone like Dr. Hammer for years and then achieved it. I know it meant a lot to you to get that job." Liam stumbled over his words. He'd never been good at this emotional connection stuff. "This must be hard. You know, for you."

Her mouth dropped open. "What are you talking about?"

"Your boss."

"Yeah, and?"

"Haven't you read a paper or seen the news?"

She pointed to the purple blotch on her cheek. "I've been busy."

Doing what was the question. The same one Liam wanted to ask, but he'd ease up for now. "Your boss is gone."

"As in?"

Oh, man. Why did he have to be the one to break this news? "The usual definition, I'm afraid."

"I still don't know what that means." Her tone got testier the longer the conversation went on. It was almost hostile now.

Liam drew in a deep breath. There was no stopping now.

"He's dead." He enunciated each word, hoping that would help the message get through to her.

She shook her head hard enough to knock a few teeth loose. "No."

"I'm sorry?"

"You're wrong."

"I am?"

"Where did you get your information about Dr. Hammer?"

Liam shrugged. "It's in the paper."

"Is my death in the paper?"

She had him there. "Well, yeah, but I was there when the police talked to Dan. They said Hammer's research is also missing. The theory is that he was killed for it."

"It's my research, too."

Liam ignored her outburst of ego. "They used some word I've never heard of to describe what you do."

"Xenotransplantation."

"It sounds like something out of a science fiction movie."

"Hardly. We can transplant organs between animal species." A new confidence filled her voice as she used her hands to act out the process. "The goal is to figure out how to grow human organs in animals and harvest them for transplants. It would eliminate the black market and organ shortages. We could offer even more than hope. We could give life."

Make that a horror flick. "Are you kidding?"

"Of course not. One of the biggest impediments relates to the human immune system, but there are ways to account for that. Success would mean no more waiting on lists for transplants or depending on artificial devices. We're talking about an epic breakthrough in the advancement of people's health. The possibilities are breathtaking."

He knew he had to put on the brakes before she gave him a full science lecture. "Anyway, the police thought you were collateral damage. That you happened to be in the building working at the wrong time."

"How did they come to that conclusion?"

"They found a body. Thought it was you at first but it turned out to be male."

Sadness pulled at the corners of her eyes. "Tom."

"Who's that?"

"The security guard." She tucked her long hair behind her ear. "Okay, so they know it's not me. What are they saying about the explosion and its cause now?"

This was not where Liam wanted the conversation to go. "They're just asking some questions. Fishing. It doesn't matter."

She ripped off a long length of paper from around the bottle. "In other words, they're blaming me."

This is what happened when a guy dealt with a brainy woman. She had this angelic face and kissable mouth, but that didn't hide the fact she was smarter than every adult around her by the time she hit the fourth grade. She didn't miss a damn thing.

"That's the new working theory," he said.

"I didn't."

He wasn't sure what to say to that since he still didn't know what happened in that building, or what was going on in her head. "Okay."

"And there's one more thing you should know."

"What's that?"

"My boss isn't dead." She took a long drink. "But when I get my hands on him, he might be."

Chapter Three

A bottle of water and two painkillers later, Maura sat on Liam's couch with him perched on the coffee table directly across from her. He hadn't really moved since they switched rooms and he crowded in, barely giving her room to breathe. He just sat there with his elbows resting on his knees and a disbelieving frown plastered across his mouth.

"One more time." His deep, husky voice broke the silence.

She forgot how potent he was up close. Dark brown hair cropped in style, and shoulders wide enough to block her view of the front door. Even in jeans and a boring shirt, danger vibrated off him. He was strong, determined and clever. Everything she needed right now. The same guy she'd avoided for years despite his friendship with Dan.

Liam's eyebrow lifted. "Maura?"

Back to reality. "The police are looking in the wrong place."

He tapped his fingertips together. "You think Dr. Hammer was kidnapped."

She wanted to believe it because the idea was better than the alternative where her boss had something to do with the fireball that consumed the lab, and nearly took her along with it. "Possibly."

"Did you recognize the people who took Dr. Hammer?"

"I saw him get into a car."

Liam sat up straighter as the gold flecks in his green eyes brightened. "I notice you're answering different questions from the ones I'm asking."

She hoped he might miss that part. Fooling him would be hard, impossible even. But until she figured out who she could trust and how to keep everyone she cared about safe, she had to be careful. "It might be smart if you stayed ignorant about some things."

He opened his arms and gestured around the room. "It's a little late for that, isn't it?"

He wasn't wrong. Sprawled on the grass with her lungs burning from the flames, she'd needed a safe house and immediately thought of him. A former undercover police officer and current corporate security expert, he was the logical choice. She depended on his sense of duty and a rock-hard loyalty to her brother to gain his cooperation.

Problem was she dragged him into her mess even though she could never hope to control him. Rather than fight, she gave him something in return for his help—information. "I heard someone in the building right before the explosion. I saw Dr. Hammer hustle out of there while I was trying not to catch on fire."

Liam shifted on the table. "So, you're saying you did see the kidnappers."

"No."

"Maura."

"I'm saying Dr. Hammer wasn't kidnapped."

Liam's face twisted in disbelief. "How do you know?"

"I just do." When Liam continued frowning, she tried again. "I have a theory and I'll find proof."

"Of what, exactly?"

She wasn't ready to give the details. "With your help."

"We're still having two different conversations."

Her mind raced ahead. She needed the documents she hid under the deck in Liam's back patio. She needed the laptop from her apartment. She needed to stay hidden while she worked out where Dr. Hammer went and why.

"We're talking about evidence," she said.

"I still don't know what we're proving."

For her investigation to work she needed to be mobile. Being interrogated could ruin everything. "No police. I'm supposed to be dead, so I'll be dead."

"Hey!" Liam clapped his hands together. "I can see your mind spinning. Stop thinking for a second and talk to me."

"How do I stop thinking?"

"I'm serious."

From the way his jaw locked, she could tell he was. To calm him back down, she slipped her palm over his hand. "Liam, I have to do this my way."

"I can't help if I don't know what the hell you're talking about."

"I need you." She'd said those same words to him nine years before. She was a kid then and he'd ignored her. Now she came to him as a woman with a problem.

He slipped his fingers through hers. "Maura…"

"You know what it took for me to ask you for anything."

He broke eye contact but stayed quiet.

"How hard it was for me to turn to you," she added.

He rubbed his thumb over her knuckles. "That happened a long time ago."

"But it's always between us."

"Doesn't have to be."

Her mind refused to go there. She couldn't afford to get sidetracked by her emotions. "Are you going to help me?"

"I still don't understand any of this."

She recognized a man on the verge of defeat. Saw the signs in his slumped shoulders and the hard lines of his face. "But you're not turning me down."

For a few seconds he just sat there. Didn't say a word. Finally he spoke. "Not this time."

LIAM STOOD IN A DARK ALLEY with his back pressed against a wall and a supposed dead woman at his side. It was a lot to take in at one in the morning. If he weren't so confused, he'd mind the crisp air. Good thing he had his frustration to keep him toasty warm.

That would teach him to let Maura set the evening agenda. He suggested she stay at the house while he made a run for whatever she needed. She could hide and he would take the risk. Since no one was looking for him, the chance of trouble was minimal. A quick and efficient strategy.

She had overruled him. Carried on about it being her life and then started talking in half sentences again. He gave in to gain a second of quiet. Now he was stuck in the middle of some sort of covert raid. The whole thing struck him as overly dramatic and unnecessary.

He followed her gaze to the third floor. "Tell me again why we're here."

"I need some of my things."

"From in there?" He pointed up at the corner window to make sure he was looking at the right place.

She nodded, her gaze never leaving her target. "It's my condo."

No lights. No movement. Ten more minutes of staring at nothing and his mind would go numb. "I think it's safe."

"The police could be in there."

"You do know I'm former police, right?"

She actually crouched down as if that would better hide her from the imaginary officers she thought were hiding in the bushes. "So?"

Liam took in her stiff shoulders and flat mouth. Determination. He couldn't argue common sense against that. "Never mind."

"I have to get my computer."

"I can buy you another one."

She glanced up at him. "This isn't about money."

"Care to clue me in on what it is about, because I still don't know."

"My hard drive. My papers." She cupped his elbow and started dragging him out into the open. "Let's go."

He had no idea what had changed and made it safe in her mind, but he wasn't about to argue. If she was ready to move, he'd lead the way.

One slide of the security key and they were in the building's downstairs glass double doors. Dead quiet greeted them. Not a surprise due to the weekday hour, but still unsettling. He expected creaks and residual condo noise. All he got was the sound of his breath whooshing in and out of his chest.

He led with a hand on his gun and her palm against his back. They stalked up the steps in an unspoken agreement not to talk. Shoes hit the stairs sending a thumping sound bouncing off the emergency stairwell walls. By the time they reached her front door, her breathing had increased. From the look of her toned body, he guessed excitement rather than exertion was the cause.

"Keys?" He held out his hand.

"What? Uh, sure." She fumbled in her pocket. Before he could stop her, she shoved the key in the lock and pushed the door open without applying any pressure.

"You don't use a bolt or anything?" he asked.

"Of course I do."

His readiness level switched to maximum. Adrenaline pumped through his veins. He breathed in deep, opening his senses to the sounds and smells of the place in the search for clues.

"Stay here." When she didn't move, he

pressed her farther down the hall and away from the door. "Not one step."

Her eyes grew to the size of plates as she whispered back to him. "Okay."

He pushed the door open with his foot and went in with his gun raised. Glass crunched under him with each step. In the shadows, he saw broken furniture and scattered papers. Keeping his back to the door and not venturing far from Maura in case she needed him, he wandered through the two-room place, ending with the small bathroom off the family room.

Nothing there but chaos and more questions.

He slipped his gun into his belt and rushed back to the entrance. He motioned for Maura to join him inside. With the door shut behind her, he turned on one small light, the one farthest away form the windows.

She came charging in, head down as if lost in thought. When her head popped up, she stopped in the dead center of the room as if she'd run into a rock wall. "What the—"

"You've been robbed."

Her mouth dropped open. "You mean searched."

"Yeah." He stood with his hands on his hips and surveyed the damage. Every drawer stood open and clothing littered the floor. He knew from experience this wasn't about a burglary. Someone had come looking for something specific. Whether they found it was the question.

What they would have done had Maura been home sent a shot of cold air ricocheting around his chest.

She circled a pile of wood on the floor that looked as if it was once a desk. "My computer is gone."

A churning started deep in his stomach. A warning of danger screamed through every pore. "We need to go."

She stopped mumbling and pacing around the disheveled room and stared at him. "Why?"

He couldn't describe the feeling. It was a sense of unease that started around his gut and rumbled up to his throat. "We just do."

Something about the look on his face must have convinced her because she dropped the paper she was holding and stepped over a pile of discarded pillows to get to him. "I'll trust you on this."

She brushed past him in her rush to get out of the room. He grabbed her arm thinking to reassure her everything was going to be okay when he heard it. The screech of sneakers against the hallway tile.

Liam touched a finger to his lips and motioned for her to move back into the kitchen. When the doorknob turned, he slid into the darkened space against the wall and next to the door. If someone came storming through, they would have to run or shoot right through him.

A second later the door pushed open, nice and slow. It never broke contact with the doorjamb, so Liam couldn't peek outside. The person didn't say anything. Didn't jerk or make any fast moves. Didn't slide his gun inside or fire off shots. He, whoever he was, was smooth. Moved without a sound.

Liam knew the type. This was the practiced lurk of a professional, someone who would kill Maura without remorse or hesitation. To keep from drawing attention or tipping off his location, Liam stayed still. The small lamp by the couch was enough of a problem. Surely, if he sensed movement in the hall, the man out there could see a light that shouldn't have been on.

Maura mouthed a word. Liam immediately understood the question. *"Police?"*

Liam shook his head in response. No, not this guy. There was nothing legitimate about what was happening here.

Liam tried to shift his weight for a better shot. The floor groaned and Maura's panicked gaze went wild with terror.

There would never be a better time. Liam threw open the door. The move left the stranger grabbing for air. Also gave Liam the two-second start he needed to knock the man's arm to the side and get him to release his weapon. But the guy didn't go down easy. He kicked out at Liam's gun and sent it skittering across the floor, then landed a sucker punch right in the center of Liam's stomach.

Doubled over with air wheezing out of his lungs, Liam dove for the other guy's midsection. Knocked him back into the wall, slamming the man's head hard against the door across the hall and sending his gun spinning. The crash sounded like an explosion on the quiet floor. No one came running, but lights flicked on under several doorways. Liam felt the shocked stares through the peepholes. He had to bring this to an end and get Maura out of there before the police streamed through.

Fists flew. Liam landed as many as he missed. This guy was quick. He dodged a left swing and kicked out, sending Liam to his knees. When the guy dove for his gun, Liam threw his arms around the man's legs and dropped him to the floor with a loud thud.

A neighbor's door opened. "What's going on out here?"

"Get back inside." Liam yelled his order through grunts and punches.

"I'm calling the police." The neighbor slammed the door as he ducked back in his condo.

"No!" Maura screamed.

Liam forced his concentration back to the man shifting and squirming beneath him. Liam was on the receiving end of a shot to the jaw that had his head rocking back and a shot of pain racing around his head. To subdue the guy and prevent another hit, Liam pounced, reaching up and screwing the man's arm behind him.

The advantage didn't last long. Using all of his weight, the guy shoved back, almost knocking Liam in a sprawl across the tile. With Liam off him, the guy tried to scoot out of reach. He slithered out from under Liam and crawled down the hall trying to use the slick tiles to pick up speed. But he couldn't get traction. After only a foot, Liam performed a second tackle. He grabbed the man's legs, avoiding a kick to the head, but just barely.

In the middle of the bruising fight, Liam saw two sneakered feet appear out of the corner of his eye. Maura stood in the danger zone.

The brief distraction gave the other man an opening. He landed his heel right under Liam's chin. The shot slammed his teeth together. Made his head spin and his vision blur. He saw a flash and then a lamp flew over his head in the direction of the other man. Maura's effort lacked a punch because the heavy end smacked against Liam's shoulder before flipping and landing on the other guy. Liam didn't even feel the punishing blow. He was too busy scrambling to his feet, trying to catch the other guy as he jumped to a standing position and bounded down the stairs at the end of the hall.

"Liam, no!" Maura called out, her voice filled with fear.

Liam ignored her desperation, fought against the urge to rush to her. He had to catch this guy or Maura wouldn't be safe.

Energy thundered through him, fueling his run and pushing out the residual twinges of pain from the fight. With his hands sliding along the banister, Liam whipped down the stairs. Heavy footsteps pounded in front of him. A shoulder slammed into the wall. The guy wasn't quiet now. The fight took care of that. Liam relished the idea he had injured the guy.

Instead of turning right and running out the front door, the man slipped to the left. The emergency alarm sounded a second later. Liam hit the landing in time to see the guy race into the dark alley. The horn blared through the building. Doors opened. People muttered. Liam felt a tug on his sleeve.

"We have to get out of here. No one can see me." Maura pleaded with him with her eyes and her voice.

Still, it took a moment for her words to register. Then he heard the yelling at the top of the stairs. Listened as the building came to life in a fury of confusion and anger.

She was right. They were out of time. "Let's go."

Chapter Four

By the time they got back to Liam's house, the police were at his front door. Only quick reflexes and expert driving skills kept them from pulling into the driveway and being seen. Liam circled the block a second time and parked the car two streets over instead.

"They followed us here?" Maura struggled to understand how her life had veered so far off course in the last two days.

"This isn't related to what happened in your condo." He got out of the car and slammed the door behind him.

Not knowing what else to do, she followed him onto the sidewalk. "How can you know that?"

"We drove straight back and they're already here. They couldn't have beaten us." He shook his head. "No, this is something else."

"You don't think it's about me?"

He stopped studying his feet. "Oh, it's definitely related to you."

"What if they're going through your house right now? If they see the—"

His eyes narrowed. "The what?"

She bit her bottom lip as she tried to figure out how much to tell him. "It's nothing, really. I mean, it matters, of course, but they won't understand what they're seeing."

"You know you've lost me, right?"

She waved her hand in front of her face. Motion helped clear her mind, and she sure needed clarity now. Without the data, figuring out Dr. Hammer's scheme and false reports bordered on impossible. That meant she'd be blamed for the fire. For a kidnapping that never happened. Dr. Hammer's work was too important to the government, too integral to NIH. They'd make an example of her. She'd lose everything.

"I need them. If the police take them, I won't be able to get them back or track this mess down." She didn't realize she spoke her thoughts out loud until she saw Liam's scrunched-up brows. "What?"

"You're talking in circles."

"I know."

"So, it's on purpose?"

She shrugged. It was either that or babble some more.

He rested his palms on her shoulders. "Look, I think I've earned the right to hear the truth. I'm following you all over the county based on your hunch."

"It's a theory."

"I'm not turning you in to the police, not talking to your brother even though I want to ease his misery." Liam massaged her tight muscles.

At his touch, her tension drained away. "I know."

"Forget the personal crap between us. For now, if you want to get out of this you've got to tell me everything."

Once he brought up their shared past, that's all she could think about. This close with his hands on her. The memories came back: being fifteen and sporting a crush on him that she mistook as love; getting rejected; retreating even further into her books and plans for the future; sacrificing all the fun of her teen years on a dream that would take her years to fulfill, and take Dr. Hammer only a short time to destroy.

This wasn't about her feelings nine years ago. This was about her career.

"There are papers at your house," she blurted out.

"I don't know what that means."

"I hid them."

"Try explaining one more time." Liam dropped his hands to his sides.

She immediately missed the warmth of his caress. Rather than mourn his touch, she shoved all thoughts about his eyes and expert fingers out of her head and concentrated on the disaster in front of her.

"I stole some documents from the lab before it went up in flames. They're at your house. Under the deck." Having that piece of information out eased the heavy weight in her stomach.

He actually smiled. "Interesting choice."

"I put them under there before you came home. Checked on them right before we left for my condo, while you were in the bathroom."

"So much for thinking I'm in charge around here."

If he needed to think that, she'd let him, but

she knew better. "You're police. You should know."

He blew out a long, ragged breath. "Let's not go back to that thing where you ask questions and make statements, and I have no idea what you're talking about."

Sometimes her thoughts bombarded her faster than she could say them. She tried to communicate, but not every sentence came out right before she moved on to something else. "Knowing what you know, would the police look there?"

"Former," he said in a distant voice as if his mind had wandered somewhere else.

"Excuse me?"

"Never mind and probably not."

Not the most comforting response, but helpful. A quick risk assessment led her to one conclusion. "I need to run. I can find a place with computer access and hack into my work account."

"Wrong."

The plan unspooled in her brain. "You can talk to the police, get a sense of what they're thinking and relay it back to me."

"Actually, I'm going to the house and you're staying here."

The words screeched to a halt on her tongue. "What?"

"You heard me."

"No way. Someone could see me. Turn me in."

He glanced at the houses around them. "It's two in the morning. Every normal human being is asleep."

It was obvious he had no intention of backing down. Fine, she'd adjust. "I'll ride in the trunk. You can pull into the driveway and I'll listen in. The conversation will probably be a bit garbled, but I should be able to follow along."

"Are you kidding?"

"If there's a chance to do it, I'll slip into the house and hide out there until you make the police go away."

Liam's eyes narrowed. "You've been watching too much television. Bad television, I might add."

She walked around to the driver's side and hit the button to pop the trunk. "This will work."

She stared into the dark, stale-smelling spot. She wasn't a fan of cramped spaces. Intellectually, she knew she'd have enough air. Common sense told her she'd be fine. Still, her heart-beat kicked up to Big Band proportions at the thought of being trapped and vulnerable. Her instincts told her to stay out and free. Ignoring that voice bellowing inside her took all of her strength.

Liam put his hand on the top of the trunk. "That is not going to happen."

As he pushed down, she pushed up. "It's the only choice."

"No, it's not. There are three hundred other ways to play this. I know you're blessed with a big brain—"

"There's some debate, but overall brain size does seem to correlate with I.Q."

"But you stink at everyday stuff. Tactics and strategies? Not where you excel."

She refused to let that insult slide. "I managed to survive a fire and save evidence."

"And along the way did something that had a guy attempt shooting his way into your condo."

Her energy spurt crashed. "That's not fair."

"I'm in charge."

She lifted her leg and scurried into the trunk as fast as possible without hurting herself. "Then start driving."

LIAM CUT THE ENGINE and swore under his breath. His unwanted guest stood at the top of the driveway, just under the sensor light. Seeing the police arrive wasn't a hardship, or even a surprise, but getting rid of this detective might be.

This was all Maura's fault. She had him driving in circles, stuffing her into his trunk and otherwise acting like a man without a drop of common sense. The more she talked, the more confused he got. And the more he wanted her.

The officer met Liam as he stepped out of the car. "It's a bit early for a visit, isn't it?"

"Where have you been?" Detective Spanner asked.

Liam knew the man. With three hundred or so people in the Alexandria Police Department, Liam had never worked with Rick Spanner, but he was the detective who showed up at Dan's house the day before. While Spanner's partner had dropped disturbing hints about Maura's part in the explosion, Spanner had played good cop. Liam wondered which role he'd try this morning.

"I've been out," Liam said.

"With anyone in particular?"

He tried not to think about Maura curled up in his car. "Do we have a problem here?"

"Why don't we move this discussion off the street and into your house?"

From the reasonable tone and calming hand gestures, Liam guessed the detective was aiming for friendly. Didn't matter to Liam since he didn't plan on talking with or trusting the guy. If he were going to tell someone about Maura, it would be Dan.

"I think we can talk just fine right here," Liam said.

"You have something to hide, Officer Anderson?"

"It's Mr. Anderson, but I think you know that." Hell, everyone knew that. It wasn't as if that part of his life stayed private. Liam had the six-inch scar on his leg to remind him every single day.

"I have some questions," Spanner said.

"At this time of the morning?"

The detective nodded as he glanced around

the front of the property. "I'd like to handle this in the least disruptive manner for you."

Yeah, sure he would. "What is the *this* again?"

"Maura Lindsey."

"What about her?"

The detective picked that moment to break off and walk around the car. "She's missing. Her boss is missing. I think you can see the problem."

"You told Dan both Hammer and Maura died in the lab."

"She is very much alive." The detective leaned with his palms flat against the hood. "There's no body, but I'm guessing that's not news to you."

"Why?"

"Not even a flicker of surprise at the idea of Maura being safe somewhere." The detective smiled. "Your lack of reaction gives you away."

Liam's mind rushed to come up with a reasonable explanation. "Your partner all but blamed Maura at Dan's apartment. False accusations seem to be the sum total of your investigation so far."

The detective slipped around the vehicle,

stopped at the trunk. "I'm trying to track her down. She could be a victim, but I can't know that until I find her."

"Ask her friends where she hangs out."

Liam sweated out every minute of the detective's casual stroll, but tried not to show any outward reaction. If the other man sensed panic, he'd be all over Liam. There was no reason for the detective to open the car or think Maura hid in there. But the man had descended on the house at this hour for a reason. Didn't take Maura's I.Q. for Liam to figure out the connection.

"She's not the social type. Her circle appears limited to the office, her brother and you."

Liam turned that comment over in his mind. That couldn't be right. How could a vibrant, beautiful young woman not have an active social life? He knew from Dan that Maura didn't date much. Dan chalked it up to a stressful and demanding job. Liam wasn't so sure.

"I'm close to Dan, not Maura."

"I'm trying to handle this before the FBI steps in." Spanner started moving again.

Liam didn't know he held his breath until it rushed out in relief at seeing the detective step away from Maura's hiding place. "Why would it?"

"An explosion in a government lab and a missing high-profile scientist? I know you're not a cop anymore, but you should be able to reason it out. Way I figure it, by tomorrow morning agents will be crawling all over this thing."

"And you don't want to lose your jurisdiction over the case to the feds."

The detective wandered around the driveway. "Something like that."

"I'm not interested in your turf war."

The detective leaned with his back to the driver's-side door. "Unless you want a whole bunch of law enforcement crawling all over your house tomorrow, I suggest we go inside and you answer some questions."

The man wasn't leaving without a fight. Liam weighed his options and decided to at least give Maura a chance to escape. He had to hope she'd run back to him once the detective left. "Fine. Let's go in."

"I knew you'd understand and come around."

Liam spared a quick glance at the trunk then conducted a visual scan of the area. He hung back and followed the detective to the front door. As soon as Spanner stepped onto the front porch, Liam aimed the key chain behind his back and hit the trunk button. Jangled his keys to hide the click, and hoped like hell she was okay in there.

PANIC SCREAMED THROUGH Maura's nerve endings. The only thing that kept her from banging on the lid and begging for release was the sweet sound of the lock disengaging. She waited for Liam to give her a signal, but he didn't pop up in front of her.

She slipped her fingers into the open space and peered out. The light at the front of the car cast the back end in shadows. The dark night kept her guessing as to who or what was out there, but she couldn't sit in the trunk one more minute. The carpet scratched her skin and the tight space had her lungs grasping for air.

Opening the trunk as little as possible, she reached her arm out and balanced her hand on the bumper. Lifting her weight up on her wrists, she slid her stomach over the edge. The rough metal edges poked her skin as she gulped in cool fresh air.

The second her feet hit the driveway she wanted to bolt. Let Liam fight this battle and slink off somewhere. Mentally regroup and develop a new plan. Tempting, but she had to clear the stain on her work. She had to rescue the findings and get them into the hands of people who would announce the discovery and give hope to truly ill people everywhere.

She hadn't sacrificed her childhood and headed off to college at fifteen, pushed herself so hard while she ignored the social aspects of her life, just to have Dr. Hammer ruin it all with his warped agenda. Whatever it was.

She crouched down behind the back fender of the car and tried to figure out what was happening inside Liam's house. She could make out figures in the front window but was too far away to hear or see anything. After a quick look around for nosy neighbors, she stayed in her bent-over position and approached the house.

Her concentration on her task broke long enough for her to pick up a mimicking sound. She took a step, and then heard another shoe crunch against the pavement off to her right somewhere. To test her theory, she tried the move again and a thud mirrored hers. Someone was out there. Someone close and quiet. The way her heartbeat pounded in her ears, she guessed the person was dangerous.

Weighing her options, she went with police over death. After a mental count to three, she took off, darting across the front lawn to the gate on the far left side. Getting the detective and Liam to notice her and come out with guns ready was the goal. She made noise, even let the gate slam shut behind her. When she heard it open again a second later, she picked up speed and rounded the back corner of the house, her sneakers sliding in the grass as her harsh breathing burned her throat.

The mad dash took her up on the patio. She body-smacked against the back glass door at a dead run. She fumbled to slide it open. When that didn't work, she pounded on it with her fist. The loud thunks grabbed the attention of both men inside.

Liam's stunned expression gave way to a fierce determination when he glanced over her head. Whatever he saw—and Maura was afraid to look around and see—made Liam shove the detective aside. He sprinted across his family room just as a beefy hand landed on her arm from behind.

She saw the stubby fingers and Liam's face. Then she saw a blur of jeans and madness as Liam threw open the door and flew over her shoulder. He smacked into her, pushing her to the side. Off balance and thrumming with energy, the move sent her to her knees on the deck. Blinding pain flooded through her but she ignored it. She was focused on the men next to her.

Liam and the intruder rolled across the grass, each trying to gain the upper hand. They came to a stop with the other man sitting on Liam's chest. A hand reached out and wrapped around his throat. Liam hit out as he coughed, bucked his hips and kicked out his legs as if attempting to shrug off the other man.

The scene registered in her brain. She had to save Liam. She struggled to stand up over the screaming aches in her legs and thumping around her temples.

"Break it up." The detective out-yelled her from his position at the back door.

Maura froze at the sound of his commanding voice. She looked at the police officer and followed his furious frown to Liam's red face.

This man could arrest her later but right now she needed him. Liam needed him.

"Do something!" She yelled the plea.

Metal flashed in the intruder's other hand. He grunted as he deflected Liam's blows. He had the size and position advantage. Pinned and choking, Liam didn't stand a chance. The man lifted his arm, bringing the knife down in an arc toward Liam's throat.

Maura opened her mouth to scream when the loud boom cracked through the night. Dog barks filled the neighborhood. She waited for lights to switch on and people to come running, but it didn't happen.

Nothing stopped the mix of horror and anguish pumping through her. "Liam!"

She rushed over just in time to see the intruder slump over Liam. Gagging and wheezing, Liam shoved at the other man's shoulders. With a lot of effort, Liam pushed the man off him then rolled to his side. He lifted up on all fours and gulped in huge swallows of air.

"Are you okay?" She rubbed his back. She wanted to comfort him, but really needed to convince herself Liam was fine. Her brain refused to believe it.

Liam nodded but didn't stop coughing.

The detective reached over the unmoving man and checked for a pulse. "Dead."

Relief flooded through her. "Good."

"Dr. Lindsey?"

At the sound of the detective's voice, the memory of where she was and why she was there came rushing back. She glanced up. "Yes?"

"I've been looking for you."

Chapter Five

Liam made a show of getting off the grass. He didn't straighten up until his hand landed on what he sought. Not that jumping to his feet would have been all that easy, anyway. The old injury on his upper thigh ached. Usually, rain set it off. Apparently, tackling a weapon-wielding assailant had the same effect.

He tried to talk over the rawness in his throat. "Let's go back inside."

The detective touched the intruder's body with the toe of his shoe. "I think you'd agree we have something to talk about now, correct?"

"Unfortunately."

Spanner stared at the body at his feet. "And I have to call this in."

Maura rushed to Liam's side and wrapped her fingers around his arm. The wildness in her eyes came out in her voice. "This is my fault. Liam isn't involved."

The detective's gaze went to her hand. "He looks pretty involved to me."

Liam wanted the other man's attention on him. Liam's plan depended on catching the detective off guard and the thing had to unfold fast. The half acre between houses wasn't enough to muffle the sound of gunshots. In this neighborhood at this time at night, someone noticed. It was only a matter of time before additional police cars showed up on his front lawn.

He knew how the process worked. Two years ago, he'd given up the law-enforcement life and switched to the less volatile world of setting up security systems at big companies and training business professionals in antikidnapping measures. The job had two benefits— it paid the bills and kept his mind working.

He was about to risk it and do the dumbest thing he'd ever done. Worse than charging into that house and risking the life of a victim and about as stupid as trying to defend his actions in the investigation and aftermath of the incident. But for Maura, he'd take another risk.

He nodded in the detective's direction. "We'll answer your questions."

Maura tightened her vise squeeze on Liam's arm. "We can't do this."

He peeled her fingers off his biceps. He needed his hands free, and her out of the way for this. "We don't have a choice here. Let's go."

Liam motioned for the detective to take the lead. He treated Maura to an almost imperceptible shake of his head when she shifted her weight as if to follow. He fell in behind the detective and waited for the right moment. Lulled in by a false sense of security and a mistaken cop-to-cop bond, the detective failed to fully protect his weapon, just as Liam had hoped.

When Spanner eased his hand off his gun, Liam moved in. He lifted his arm and touched the tip of the intruder's knife against the detective's neck. He jumped in surprise, wincing as the knife nicked him.

Before the man's instincts kicked in, Liam reached around and took his gun. "Huge mistake."

"What the—"

Liam pressed the blade tighter against the

other man's skin. "Didn't the academy instructors teach you not to turn your back on a suspect?"

"What are you doing?" Maura asked in a flat voice that mirrored the blank look on her face. "This is nuts."

"Listen to the lady." Spanner tried to shake his head but his flesh met with the sharp edge.

Liam ignored them just as he ignored the voice in his head that told him to come up with another plan. "Shut up."

"Not smart, Anderson."

"Maybe." More like definitely, but Liam didn't see a choice here. Not now. He needed Maura with him to hunt down Dr. Hammer. Liam steered the detective into the house before the man figured out he should start yelling for help.

"This is not the way you want to go out." Gone was the baiting. Spanner now talked in textbook cop-speak. Calm and controlled. No show of fear.

"I'm already out. You know that."

Maura rested her hand against the small of Liam's back. Whispered into his ear. "Maybe we should talk about this.

"I know you like plans, but I've got this under control." And he didn't want the detective thinking he could divide and conquer.

She brushed her fingers down his cheek and gave him a sad smile. "I hope so."

Spanner kept his hands raised but didn't hide the fact he listened in. "What can you gain here?"

"Time." Liam grabbed the radio off the other man's belt and checked it. Last thing he needed was a broadcast of the assault over the police frequencies.

"I can help you get whatever you need."

"How about the truth?"

"Sure," Spanner said in a practiced, calm tone. "Tell me what you think that is."

Liam recognized the training. No way would that strategy work. He pointed at his kitchen chair. "Sit."

Spanner froze in place. The man was smart enough to know he should stay on his feet. "No."

"I'm the one with all the weapons," Liam said.

"You're not going to hurt me."

"Don't be so sure." He tightened his grip on

the detective's arm. "In a contest between you and her, she'll win every time."

Maura moved around the detective, making sure not to get within striking distance, and faced both men. "Liam, what do you want me to do?"

"Ma'am, this is a mistake."

She lifted her chin, stared straight into Liam's eyes. "I trust Liam, not you."

Her words renewed his belief that this was the best way to go. She needed a savior. He'd failed in that role before—hell, he'd failed *her* before—but this time could be different.

Liam hooked his foot under the bottom bar of the chair and pulled it out. It screeched against the floor. "You being here and accusing her is the problem. Maura didn't cause the explosion."

"Then let me help you prove that." Spanner focused on Maura. Pitched his voice nice and low. Took on a soothing I-can-help persona.

"I'm impressed with your officer training. You do the *let's be friends* thing pretty well. But I know how this works because I took the same classes. She goes to jail and then we're stuck."

Spanner shook his head. "Your girlfriend

can get out on bail. But not if you pull this stunt. Let me go now and we'll pretend this never happened."

Maura nibbled on her lower lip. "Liam, maybe you should listen to him. I don't want you in this much trouble."

"He's lying." The choice had been made. It was too late now. "I'm holding a gun on a police officer. Trust me, he's not going to forget it. The entire department will jump on me for this one."

"Not true." The detective sounded sincere, but his cold eyes hinted to the anger bubbling just under the surface. "We have an understanding. You're former police. I've seen your file. You were decorated and got a bad rap. We all know it."

Liam wondered when Spanner would get around to that form of bargaining. "So, now we're friends?"

"I know what it's like to have a woman turn your head."

Maura snapped out of her stunned state. "That is not what this is about."

Spanner shrugged. "Then tell me."

"No." Liam knew if he let her launch into her science speech they'd never get out of there. Worse, Spanner would know where to start looking. Liam didn't want to give the other man that much of an advantage. "We're going to tie you up and take off."

Spanner shook his head. "You're walking into a lot of trouble. I wasn't kidding about the feds."

Through all of the other lies, Liam recognized that bit as fact. "That's why we need to go now."

"Ma'am, talk some sense into him."

Enough talking. "Maura?"

"Yes, Liam?"

"Grab the detective's handcuffs."

PATRICIA HAMMER PACED around Rick Spanner's office a few hours after his fellow officers released him from the kitchen chair. He was tired and more than a little pissed that he let Liam get the jump on him. Having to deal with the paperwork about the incident and babysit an irate trophy wife only made the situation worse.

He knew the jokes from his fellow detectives would come later. Liam would pay for that alone.

Patricia's high heels clicked against the

tile and her thin skirt inched up with every step. Spanner assumed some men found the fake-tan, big-boobs type attractive. To him, she looked like a predator. Being fifty and married, he wasn't impressed with the type of woman who picked her husband by his bank account. Mrs. Hammer struck him exactly as that woman.

She stopped on the other side of his desk and tapped her long nails against the wood. "How did you let the woman get away?"

He inhaled for the third time. The first happened when his boss asked the same question. "Dr. Lindsey has help."

"Some washed-up former police officer."

Looked like on top of everything else, Dr. Hammer's wife was the judgmental type. "A man who knows how to use a gun."

"This is unacceptable."

Spanner actually agreed with that part. "We'll get her. She doesn't have that many options."

"You don't know that. Someone could have paid her to blow up the building." Mrs. Hammer waved her hand in the air in a dismissive gesture. "She could have backing or resources."

"Not the woman I saw."

"You mean the same woman who was smart enough to escape while you were watching her?" Mrs. Hammer stabbed her finger into the desk.

He ignored the shot to his ego. "Right now, it's equally as likely she's another victim."

"Ms. Lindsey killed my husband."

"Doctor."

"What?"

"Dr. Lindsey and we don't know if she killed anyone." From what he'd seen, Maura followed directions well and everyone kept talking about her big brain. He could see her pulling this off. He just didn't know where she put Dr. Hammer since the guy wasn't at Liam's house. "There is no evidence to suggest your husband is dead."

"He is. I can feel it."

Spanner doubted the Hammers had the romantic connection the woman tried to portray. Her husband worked for the government, yes, but he had written several books and won many prestigious professional prizes. From Spanner's research, the man did just fine in the income department. Maybe he didn't earn enough to keep this woman happy, but they sure could live comfortably.

"Your husband is considered missing."

"You have twenty-four hours to find her."

"Ma'am?"

"The FBI is supposed to take over today. I give you all one day to figure this out before I go to the newspapers."

"And say what?"

"Offer an award to bring in Ms. Lindsey."

"You mean a bounty?"

"That sounds accurate."

The thought of vigilantes roaming the streets tracking a young scientist sent an icy-cold wave washing over him. "That's not wise."

"You have a choice."

"Which is?"

"You handle it or I will."

Chapter Six

Maura sat on the motel-room bed with papers spread out in front of her and Liam's laptop off to the side. The information Dr. Hammer submitted to NIH differed from the documents she'd drafted. Looking back now, every time she completed an interim report on their research, he edited it to falsify the findings. The document copies she had didn't match anything he submitted to his superiors.

"Any clearer?" The mattress dipped when Liam eased his leg on to the edge.

"Less, actually."

"Maybe Hammer thought he had to lie about the results in order to keep the money flowing. You know, make things sound better than they were."

"That's not it."

"Once he feared you might be onto him, he

had no choice but to destroy everything or risk being caught."

Her mind ran in the exact opposite direction. False reports. Inaccurate findings. It all pointed to Dr. Hammer trying to ruin his work. She had no idea why he would do something like that. "No."

"No?"

She shuffled through the stacks, sending papers flying in every direction. "I'm missing something. Something outside of NIH."

"You lost me." Liam picked some pages off the floor and added them to the pile in front of her. "Again."

"You're making the wrong assumptions. We were successful." The news used to fill her with unbelievable satisfaction. She woke up and rushed to the lab just to get started again. She couldn't focus on anything else.

Now it was all tainted.

Liam exhaled hard enough to rock the mattress. "Since I don't know anything about your work except the parts I already want to forget, you need to explain this in a more basic way."

All of her research was top secret, owned by the government and subject to release at its discretion. She had no right to talk about the work, but Dr. Hammer's actions changed everything. "We did the impossible. We grew human organs for harvesting."

"The animal thing."

"Transplanting organs from—"

"Stop." Liam held up his hand. "I'm with you. Well, not really, but at least I understand what topic we're discussing."

"The point is we didn't fail." Energy pounded through her at the thought. She remembered those initial moments of pure discovery when she saw the beginnings of the cure for diabetes.

"How could Hammer not understand that?"

"He did. The man is brilliant. He had trained his entire life in this field. Of course he understood the gravity and importance."

Liam used his thumb to flip through the pile closest to him. "Then something else is going on."

"Except for his choice of a wife, Dr. Hammer was so practical."

"We don't like her?"

Maura heard the smile in Liam's voice, saw the tug at the corner of his mouth. "She's all about makeup and shoes. Really not his type at all."

Liam looked at Maura then. "You'd be surprised what men like."

Why should today be any different? She spent her entire life trying to care about the things other people cared about. And men? There was a topic she had very little experience in. Almost none, actually. She'd tried to live the moments others talked about, but her plans never worked. Not the one with Liam, and not many others.

Rather than dissect all the ways her social life went astray, she stuck to the topic of Dr. Hammer. "If he got on a path it could be days before I heard him do anything but mumble."

Liam's smile fell. "Sounds crazy."

"He's a dedicated genius."

"You sure that's not an excuse?"

Liam's words hit her like a smack to the face. "Do you think I'm crazy?"

"I think you're strong and beautiful and in a hell of a lot of trouble."

She wanted to ignore the last one and concentrate on the others, but she couldn't. "Which is the reason I have to figure out why

Dr. Hammer would say his work was flawed when it wasn't."

Liam nodded as he glanced around the bed. "I'll take a look."

"No offense, but you don't understand the science."

"Not even a little, but we don't need additional I.Q. points on this. We need to figure out what doesn't fit."

"Isn't that what I said?"

"Not that I could tell."

"Why do you think you're qualified to…" She stopped when Liam's eyebrow lifted. "Never mind."

She winced over the shortness of her tone. Dan warned her about her tendency to brush aside suggestions and sound superior. She never saw herself that way and she didn't want others to, either.

"I can read, you know," Liam said.

"I didn't mean it that way."

"My father was a college professor. He kind of insisted I go to school now and then."

That news wiped out all of the other thoughts ricocheting through her brain. "A professor?"

"Yeah."

For years, she'd made a concentrated effort to know as little about Liam's personal life as possible. It was the best way for her to stay disconnected from him and keep an emotional distance. The teenage version of her hadn't cared about his parents. The grown-up version felt a flood of sympathy for Liam when Dan explained how Liam's dad suffered a heart attack at the desk in his office. The death had hit Liam hard since he'd lost his mother to breast cancer when he was very young. Maura related to the loss of a parent since an accident had grabbed both of hers and left her reeling.

"What did your dad think about you being a cop?" she asked.

"Not much."

From Liam's no-nonsense tone, she'd expected that answer. "He wanted you to follow in his footsteps?"

"Guns didn't really have a place in his world."

She tried to come up with a good way to discuss this subject. "I'm sure he was proud of what you accomplished."

"Not really." Liam finally met her gaze head-on. "He died one week after I was suspended from the police force."

The stormy pain behind his eyes made her heart ache for him. "I'm sorry."

He grabbed a handful of papers. "These are the documents with references to places other than NIH. If you're trying to get an idea of what Hammer was doing outside of NIH, this is the best place to start."

A dark heaviness moved into her chest. The sharing took her mind off her job and the mess her life had become. For a few precious seconds, having that weight lifted brought relief. After years of running from Liam, running with him felt right.

But as quickly as the window into his life opened, he shut it again. She wasn't sure if she'd get another peek into what made Liam the man he was. After pushing him away, avoiding him, she wasn't sure she deserved another chance.

"Hammer consulted with experts at Lancaster Labs, Smithfield Enterprises." Liam flipped through the pages. "Should I go on?"

"Can I stop you?"

"I'm a security expert. I have the resources to track these leads down. Do a bit of snooping."

"Like how?"

He tapped the end of her nose. "You've got your big brain. Information is my secret weapon, gathering it and analyzing it."

"Can you tap into the government's computers?"

"Of course."

She eyed him up, not sure whether to believe him. He sounded pretty confident. From everything Dan said about him, Liam had contacts everywhere and spent a lot of time figuring out how to get into places other people couldn't access. Not the most legal skill set, but probably very helpful for what she had in mind.

He sighed at her for about the fifteenth time during the conversation. "Look, all I'm saying is that you probably can't see the one wrong turn because you're on top of the information. You read through and see your boss's lies and spin off from there."

In a flash she switched from hopeful to insulted. She'd spent her entire life trying to overcome preconceived notions. Her age. Her gender. Some people even claimed she was too pretty to work in science. She despised the stereotypes.

"I am perfectly capable of reviewing documents," she pointed out, not even trying to hide the anger in her voice.

He had the nerve to smile at her. "You are too emotional on this."

"That's ridiculous. I'm focused and determined and, and…"

He caught her hand in midwave and trapped it against his leg. His thumb drew a lazy pattern over her knuckles as his lips turned up in that sexy little way that had gotten to her since she was in high school.

"We'll both look," he suggested.

"I still don't see—" The words got trapped in her throat when he cupped her cheek in his palm.

"Tell me something."

"What?" The question came out as little more than a whisper.

"Is the offer from nine years ago still open?"

She pulled her hand away from him. "Is that supposed to be funny?"

"Of course not."

She pushed up and off the bed. Sitting near him at the moment filled her with a killing heat. "I was a teenager."

"And I was eight years older, in my twenties."

"So?"

"You were off-limits back then."

"You made your opinion quite clear." She folded her arms across her stomach.

"Admittedly, I could have handled the situation better."

"Gee, you think?"

"I was a kid myself. Ravaged by hormones and dumb about women. You were a guaranteed way to get my butt kicked or to land in jail. I didn't get smarter until many years later."

"Is that what you are now?"

"I'm determined."

She wasn't sure how to respond to that except to get as far away from him as possible. "I need a shower."

"Excuse me?"

"I think best in the shower."

"We were talking about us."

"There isn't any us."

Liam sighed. "I see you're still running from me."

"You're not the only one who's learned a few things over the years."

RICK SPANNER LEFT LIAM'S study for last. He had searched every other room in the house. Despite having a vibrant security business, the man didn't have an actual office. As far as Spanner could tell, the business property consisted of a five-screen computer setup and a walk-in safe.

A locksmith was on his way over to break the combination, but the man didn't sound too reassuring. Once he heard the make of the six-foot metal structure, the locksmith suggested Spanner find Liam because that would be easier than getting the door open.

But Spanner knew he didn't have that kind of time. The feds had moved in and were working the case. High-ranking government officials checked in almost hourly about Dr. Hammer and his findings. Whatever this man did, it was damn important.

Spanner sank into the tall desk chair and stared at the keyboards. He enjoyed computers, but not being a technology wizard, he was way out of his league. Normally, he would call in the experts on his team and let them comb through the computer hard drives looking for whatever might provide a clue as to Liam's location. Spanner didn't have that luxury today. He was officially off the case. It was one thing for him to put his career on the line. It was something else to insist that a colleague do the same.

Hitting one space bar brought the entire system to life. Also showed the lack of password protection. The choice didn't make much sense for a guy who paid the mortgage based on his expertise. Spanner figured Liam left in a hurry and without locking down his system. That's what happened when you kidnapped a police officer and fled the scene. Spanner refused to feel sorry for Liam's bad choices.

A few clicks and he got to the most interesting programs, the ones separated for the security business. He wasn't sure what he was looking for other than any hint as to where Liam might have taken Maura.

Spanner opened the business files, and the screens flipped to a bright blank blue. "What the hell?"

He tried to escape and restart, but the

screens didn't change. Then the countdown began. In the lower right corner, a counter ticked off the files as the system deleted them. When shutting off and rebooting didn't work, he banged on the keyboard. Then swore. Anything to make the file destruction stop. The more options he tried, the faster he lost the information.

Finally, he gave up and leaned back in his chair. It looked as if Liam knew what he was doing, after all. That made him very dangerous.

Chapter Seven

Maura turned off the lights and slipped into bed after a day spent bent over documents. She didn't even ask Liam if he was done reading the pile of papers in front of him. He wasn't, but she stuck to her schedule anyway.

Since she stepped out of the bathroom an hour before, she'd been almost embarrassed. She avoided eye contact and focused on the papers. When he started a conversation, she brushed him off with a noncommittal "hmm" without lifting her head.

He wanted to tell her he turned down her offer all those years ago for some noble purpose. Truth was he was a self-important kid who didn't want to get bogged down with any girl from his hometown. His professor father spent years trying to drag him out of football and into more worthy pursuits like chess club. Liam felt the disapproval every single day. He wanted out of the house before he suffocated.

Having the science-geek sister of his best friend ask him to rid her of her virginity was well outside of his life plan. She was too young and naive. He wanted a woman with experience.

He associated being smart with being boring, with stifling and judging him. Sure, he could have let her down easy, told her she was special and that she should wait until she was in love. Instead, she surprised him and he laughed at her.

The memory nagged him. It came back to him now and then. He owed her an apology and an explanation. She had been backward and his harsh words sent her even deeper into her studies. As far as he knew, she never shared their secret. Dan certainly didn't know, and Liam had no intention of filling him in.

When he looked at her now he saw a different person. A woman. Still shy and almost awkward in a social setting, but beautiful and loyal and everything a man could want a woman to be. Now that he was older he appreciated smart, even though her level of smart scared the hell out of him. It made him feel unworthy, like that underachieving boy who preferred the outdoors to the family library, but that was his issue.

He owed her more than innuendos and drooling stares. He had to make this right.

He stared at the lump in the bed. Somehow she managed to take up most of the double mattress. He guessed she wanted him to sleep on the floor. That wasn't going to happen.

Without taking off his clothes, and careful not to scare her, he slid into bed next to her. He stayed on top of the covers. The idea of her waking up screaming didn't appeal to him. He also needed to make sure they didn't call attention to themselves. Her photo already had shown up on the news as a potential witness in the explosion. Liam knew that was code for suspect.

He had waited to see his picture in connection with the assault on Spanner. That one hadn't made the news yet, which bought them maybe a day of time.

He wrapped an arm around her and anchored her body back against him. Layers of blanket and sheet separated them, but he could still feel the heat of her skin. This close, the smell of her shampoo filled his nose. Floral and feminine. Just as he had dreamed.

"What are you doing?" She mumbled the question into the pillow.

He kissed the line where her hair lay against her cheek. "I hoped it would be obvious."

"No, I'm serious." She turned around so fast that he actually fell on top of her for a second. "What is this?"

He shoved up, balancing his body on his elbow. As much as he wanted to touch skin against skin, he refrained. For now.

"I'm not forcing you," he said.

"I didn't say you were." She pulled the sheet tight against the base of her neck. "But what's happening here?"

He took in the wide eyes and stress lines around her mouth. Hardly the look of a woman hoping for seduction. "Are you afraid of me?"

"I already told you no."

He wasn't convinced. "Then why the panic?"

Her startled gaze scanned his face. "I'm not used to being pawed."

"Pawed?"

"Can't you sleep on the floor?"

"Tell me what's really going on in your head." He touched his finger to her lips. "What has you so spooked?"

"Dr. Hammer."

The revving up in Liam's gut slammed to a halt. "You're actually talking about the office now."

"I just don't see his motivation. He has prestige and grants. NIH would have given him anything he asked for. What's missing?"

Liam wondered if anything ever mattered to her more than the job. "I don't know."

She folded her arms over the top of the blanket, giving him a peek of bare shoulders and tiny straps of material holding whatever covered her. "I've been thinking."

"Me, too."

He didn't telegraph or ask permission. He just leaned down and pressed his mouth against her soft lips. One small touch, only a few seconds and barely moving, and then he lifted his head.

Or that was the plan. He hadn't counted on how good she'd feel or how much he'd want to keep on kissing her.

Slowly, giving her time to pull back, his lips met hers again. This kiss did more than linger. It went deep and long. His mouth traveled over hers as he learned her taste. Licking his tongue over her lips, he had her lifting her head, wanting him back.

Heat radiated off her. Small mumbling sounds filled her throat.

Losing himself in her felt good. Right.

He shifted until his hands brushed against her cheeks and his fingers tangled in her long hair. Lifting his body, his chest over hers, he pushed her into the mattress. With every pass of his lips, the need to take her grew stronger. A voice in his brain told him to go slow. Reminded him that her mind flew in a million directions and all of them led to work. Getting her to focus on him might take longer than he could bear.

He didn't know her level of experience, but he assumed she was slim in that department. She'd gone to college before she could drive, finished graduate school before she could legally drink. That sort of detachment from her age group had an impact.

But, damn, the woman could kiss. The way her arms folded around him and her fingers brushed up his back, he knew she wasn't afraid. For a few seconds, her focus was on him and he wasn't about to let that get past him.

Sliding along the sheets, he moved down until his lips found her jawline. He kissed in a line until his mouth hovered at the base of her neck. Her skin smelled sweet, like bunches of flowers. It was the same scent that hit him when she threw the bathroom door open earlier. He didn't know what was in those motel bottles, but it turned to sweetness on the rounded tops of her breasts.

She switched from skimming her fingers through his hair to yanking on a few strands. "Smithfield Enterprises," she mumbled against his forehead.

From the combination of tugging and nonsense words, his head shot up. "What?"

"That's it."

Even in the darkness he could see her bright smile. That didn't mean he had any idea what was happening. "What the hell are you talking about?"

She shoved against his shoulders. "Get up."

"Now?"

Her face went blank when she lifted her hips

and pressed her lower body hard against his. "Oh."

"Yeah, oh."

"You're a good kisser."

"Apparently not good enough to keep your mind from traveling all over the place."

"But you did it."

"Uh, no, but I was trying to."

She waved him off. At this distance, she actually smacked her hand against his chin by accident. "It was something you said."

"My mouth was busy doing something other than talking."

"I'm not kidding."

He couldn't believe she didn't notice how serious he was. "Let me get this straight. We were all over each other, kissing and touching and getting into it, and you're stopping to talk about your boss."

She gnawed on her lower lip. "Is that weird?"

"A little bit, but strangely, I'm not surprised." He shifted his weight, feeling each warmed muscle groan in frustration as he left her.

"I'm sorry. My mind tends to run ahead—"

"I know."

"Really?"

If she bit down any harder on her lip she'd bite it off. Since he'd grown pretty fond of that part of her anatomy in the last few seconds, he kissed her to get her to stop. Quick and, he hoped, reassuring.

He reached over and turned on the light. Once he saw her all snuggled in the covers with skin flushed pink from their intimacy, he had to battle back the need to touch her again. "Now, fill me in on what I said to get you to stop rubbing your hands all over me."

"I wasn't doing that."

Despite her disgruntled facial expression, he shot her his best you've-got-to-be-kidding-me look. "Just explain."

The cloudy confusion in her eyes cleared. "You mentioned Smithfield Enterprises."

"When?"

"Not important." She scooted up until her back rested against the headboard. "The point is Smithfield was not included in the reports to NIH."

"Am I supposed to know what that means?"

"Dr. Hammer was supersecretive, almost paranoid about his research, but other labs and companies have government funding and contracts and do pieces of work that fit together with ours. At NIH's request, he frequently consulted with those places. In turn, the records to NIH are supposed to detail every meeting with other experts, every time Dr. Hammer spoke or lectured anywhere."

"So far that all makes sense."

"When I drafted the interim reports, I included our contacts with Smithfield Enterprises."

The answer smacked him right in the forehead. "But the ones Dr. Hammer turned in omitted the meetings with the company."

She pointed at him. "Exactly."

"Told you I wasn't dumb."

She patted him on the knee. "Never said you were."

Since he doubted she realized when she veered into condescending territory, he ignored that. "What does Smithfield do?"

"Biotech. Lots of work in the immunology field. That plays into handling the downsides of our work in transplantation."

He rolled his eyes. "So many big words."

"You're the one spouting off about your intellect."

"True." At least he now had somewhere to start looking. "Now it's my turn."

"To do what?"

"Check into Smithfield Enterprises."

LANGDON HAMMER APPRECIATED his new lab. It occupied most of one floor of a multi-story office building. If he wanted something, he asked one of the guards and whatever it was appeared after a series of security measures were disengaged and a huge metal door swung open.

The only problem was the lack of a true assistant. Since he wasn't supposed to be there, wasn't supposed to be alive, he spent his days alone and his nights in the suite of rooms off the lab. He didn't mind the quiet because it allowed him to concentrate at the level he needed to finish his work. But he still preferred the setup he had with Maura. She did her tasks and stayed out of his way. It was the perfect relationship.

After a series of beeps, the pressure lock opened. Steady footsteps rang out, warning of the approach. "Dr. Hammer. I need a few minutes of your time."

His hands froze in the middle of putting on

his gloves. Refusing to show fear, he turned around and faced his visitor.

"Of course." It wasn't as if he had a choice but to have the conversation.

Tall and dark with the deadest black eyes of any living creature on the planet, Rex Smithfield could scare even the toughest guards in the building. Dr. Hammer knew because he'd watched panic wash over huge men with even bigger guns whenever anyone even mentioned Smithfield's name.

The man in question shook his wrist as he adjusted his cuffs. "Unfortunately, this is about Dr. Lindsey again."

"What about her?"

"It would appear she is missing."

Locked away from news and other people, Dr. Hammer assumed Maura had died in the fiery explosion at the lab. This was the first clue he had that something went wrong that night. "I thought you were going to…"

"Yes?"

Dr. Hammer swallowed at the lifeless tone to the other man's voice. "Take care of the issue."

"Dr. Lindsey has proven to be more resourceful than we initially anticipated."

Smithfield leaned against the counter with his arms crossed in front of him. "Which brings me to my question. I need to know what information the woman has about your ties to me."

Dr. Hammer noticed Smithfield didn't even bother with a question. He went straight to flat-toned fury. "Nothing."

"I would warn you that lying to me is not the way to handle this situation."

The tension in the room threatened to suffocate him. "Nothing more than the ordinary course for a lab assistant. She entered my consultation data into her interim reports, so she knows about my meetings here and at other places."

Smithfield's grim frown spoke for him.

"That was before we reached our agreement," Dr. Hammer explained. "I've erased all the references to Smithfield since then."

"That means she knows to look here for answers."

"I wouldn't say that."

Smithfield's fingers tightened against his black suit jacket. "You insist she is brilliant, correct?"

"Yes."

"Then she will start with what doesn't fit."

He was a scientist not a military tactician. He depended on Smithfield and his men to control the situation so he could focus on his experiments. In any other circumstance he would order and dictate, remove everyone from his presence. Those strategies didn't work with Smithfield.

Dr. Hammer knew he had to watch every word and keep all of his boiling anger tamped down. A wrong move and Smithfield could crush him. He was a man who got his way and paid good money to ensure he controlled every situation. He owned Dr. Hammer, and Dr. Hammer knew it.

"Is she talking to the police?" he asked.

"Currently, she is running from them to avoid being arrested for your disappearance."

"That kind of activity doesn't sound like her."

"There is a man with her."

Dr. Hammer wondered how any of this could be possible. "With Maura?"

"You assured us we only had to worry about her brother."

The icy edge to Smithfield's voice sent a

chill through Dr. Hammer. "That was my understanding."

"You were wrong." Smithfield stayed scarily still. No part of him moved as he offered his explanation. "This man is a security expert."

"I don't know who that could be."

"He is someone who could unravel our delicate relationship." Smithfield stared at the ceiling as if it were the most interesting thing in the world. "Do you know what that means?"

Dr. Hammer rushed to reassure Smithfield before he got an idea to end their arrangement the hard way. Through the worst type of termination. "We can control her."

Smithfield lowered his chin and aimed an arctic stare at Dr. Hammer. "That was your promise, yes, but we need to find her first."

It was as if all of the warmth and air sucked out of the room. Being this close to a man who wielded the power to wipe his existence from the Earth rattled Dr. Hammer's nerves. He was not the type of person who worried about his place in the world...except when under Smithfield's watch.

"I don't know where she could be."

Smithfield's eyebrow lifted. "That is unfortunate."

Chapter Eight

Liam walked into the towering three-story glass lobby of Smithfield Enterprises at noon the next day. Fancy artwork hung on the marble walls. Leather chairs sat around the area in what he assumed was supposed to be an inviting arrangement. Since no one used them, he had his doubts about the look. It all struck him as cold and lifeless, but he wasn't there to admire the decor.

Using fake credentials he copied after studying the real ones, Liam walked past the welcoming woman at the visitor's desk after giving her a good-morning nod. All of twenty with a wide smile and perfect, straight white teeth, she beamed with happiness back at him.

The two six-foot paid killers behind her didn't share her enthusiasm. The one with the shaved head and snarl stepped in front of him, blocking his path to the elevator bank. "You need to check in."

Liam lifted his badge from where it was hooked to his belt. "I work here."

The guard nodded toward the reception desk. "Everyone checks in until we say otherwise."

So much for thinking working around the metal detector, keypad and sensor screen that validated the chip in his badge would get him in. "Sure."

"May I help you?" the young woman asked with a false enthusiasm that had him wondering what she'd sound like after a few more years standing there.

"I'm new here."

"Well, welcome to the building. Let me just check you in so you don't have to stop here every day."

"Do all employees stop here?"

The woman's smile faltered. "Only the first few times. Those are the rules."

She sat back in her seat and started typing. Liam knew everything would check out because he set up the identity. Breaking into Smithfield's internal system proved impossible.

The company had its private information in complete lockdown, kind of like Liam's own closed-access, hard-to-crack program. The professional in him appreciated the effort. That same part of him also looked for another way in and found it.

Smithfield contracted out part of its tech work to a staffing company. From what he could tell, a group of workers sat in the basement and stayed segregated from the Smithfield group except when a problem arose. The tech guys didn't work on confidential projects other than to keep the building's significant technical components working.

This should have shut Liam down, but he found a loophole. The tech group linked to its home office for administrative things like payroll. The arrangement turned out to be very hackable. Liam could only get in through the tech system on a limited basis, but it was enough to give him access to the badge information and provide cover by adding his fake credentials to the approved list of workers.

The woman's eyebrows pushed together as she typed. After a few clicks, her smile returned. She handed his badge back. "Welcome to Smithfield Enterprises. Your office is one floor down on the mezzanine level."

That didn't much matter to him since he planned to go up. "Thanks."

He got two steps before Maura's voice whispered in his ear through the tiny microphone dot he placed there. "She's pretty."

He smiled at the jealous sting to her voice. To hide his private discussion and prevent people from thinking he talked to himself, he mumbled under his breath. "A little young for me, don't you think?"

"I forgot you're not a fan of young women."

He ignored the jab. "I prefer the brainy running-from-the-police type these days."

"You are a smart man."

He adjusted his tie. The implanted camera allowed her to see every move he made. At the elevator, he slid his key card through the reader then pressed the up button.

"After everything you had to do to get in the building they wouldn't just let you go upstairs?" she asked.

"Nope. There are a series of protective measures in place." He couldn't help but be impressed. "It's smart security."

"Sounds like overkill. Biotech firms specialize in that sort of thing. You'll never meet anyone more paranoid than a research scientist."

"Keeps the unwanted out."

"You mean, like you?"

"Guess that didn't work, did it?" He nodded to the people exiting the car when the doors opened. After it emptied out, he stood in there all alone and waited for the door to slide shut again. "Guide me around the area using the blueprints."

"The steel reinforced area we want to check out is on the fifth floor." The microphone picked up the sounds of crinkling papers. "The main labs are on other floors, but that's too obvious."

"Hard to imagine Smithfield would be dumb enough to stick Hammer—a guy who is supposed to be dead or kidnapped—in with all of the other scientists in the building."

"That would make containment hard."

"Then five it is." He hit the button. After a rumble, the car went down instead of up. He spun around and pounded on the up arrow, trying to send the car in the direction he wanted.

"You're moving around and I'm getting dizzy. What's going on?" she asked.

"We have trouble." He lifted the tie so she could see the descending numbers above the door through the small camera.

She chuckled. "You hit the wrong button."

"No, I didn't."

She cleared her throat. "Are you sure?" The amusement had left her voice.

That familiar churning started in his gut. "It's possible the key-card chip determines your floor access."

The M button flashed and the elevator didn't stop.

"So much for the floor theory." He mumbled the comment over the tapping in his earpiece. Sounded like the beat of a pen against a desk.

"Where did you get that chip?" she asked.

"From the security guard while he was having lunch yesterday. I recreated mine. There shouldn't be any restrictions."

"Get out of there." Her words came out in a frantic rush.

He had the same thought but the execution was the problem. "How am I supposed to do that when I'm in a moving elevator?"

"Where is it going?"

"Underground. Looks like one of the basement levels."

"There are seven of them, including three for the garage."

He watched as numbers for each floor lit up as he passed. The car lowered to the bowels of the building. He got a flash of his future and it included walking off the car and into an ambush of gunfire.

The only solution was far from perfect. He slammed his palm against the emergency button. The quick stop threw him against the back of the elevator. He waited for an alarm to sound but the small box stayed deathly quiet.

"What are you doing?" she asked in a shaky voice.

"Getting out of here while I can still walk."

"You think it's a setup?"

Not think. Knew with a certainty that rocked him to the core. "They figured out the badge was a fake."

"How is that possible? You were so careful." Her words jumbled together.

For some reason he took unexpected comfort

in her sudden lack of control. "These guys are good."

"Can you be impressed another time? I'm betting the bruising security guys can pry the doors open with their fingertips."

Liam worried they could kill with them. "True."

He looked around. The only ways out of this situation were through the doors or the ceiling. Both options sucked. He gambled on only one being protected by armed men.

With one hand planted against the wall, he used the handrail for leverage and jumped up, knocking the ceiling panel out. The plastic cover crashed to the marble floor. The crack sounded like an explosion in the small space.

"What the heck was that?" She screamed the question.

The high-pitched shriek bulleted right into his brain. "Damn, woman."

"What did I do?"

"Forget it." He closed his eyes and waited for someone to rappel down on top of him. Instead of feeling relieved, he questioned his luck. He had a load of problems ahead of him.

First there was the camera. Someone watched all of this, which lessened his already poor chances of getting out of there without being arrested or killed. The second was that the cover came off too easy. In Liam's world, effortless meant trouble. And there was the issue of his luck. The last time he'd tried to rescue a woman, he'd ended up with two shots in his thigh and an official reprimand. Reliving that experience didn't appeal to him.

"How are you going to get up in that hole?" she asked.

Good question. "Use my awesome strength."

"I can work out the right angle for the best lift, if you want."

"No, I got this."

Guys on television did this sort of dead-lift thing all the time, but the reality was much harder. Having Maura watch might help. After all, what man liked to fall flat on his face in front of his woman? And that's how he thought of her right now. Smart, stunning and tough. If he lived through this and managed to stay out of jail, he'd work on having that impressive mind focus on him for more than ten minutes at a time.

He jumped again, this time grabbing on to the edge of the opening. He hung there for a second. Much longer and his muscles would fatigue too fast. He had to hoist his body up there now. His second hand joined the first. Using all of his strength, he performed the world's hardest chin lift and he did it in a suit with an audience. Why he forgot to take off the jacket first was a mystery.

His head cleared the opening. With one last burst of energy, he slid his arms onto the ledge. Just as he got his balance, the car started moving. His left arm slipped as gravity pressed him back down.

"Now what happened?" she asked.

"Time ran out."

He struggled and shifted until he got his hand back up and his legs through the hole. A few more pushes and grunts and he got to his feet.

Standing on the top of a moving elevator didn't give him many options. The dark, humid area didn't exactly have any emergency exit signs. Cables held the car and ran twenty stories into the air. There were openings on each of the four sides. He assumed they led out to the hallways.

When he looked down, he saw he only had two floors left to plan an escape. That meant jumping into one of the openings that raced by him as the car moved down. He didn't wait. With his arms up, he leaped for the closest one. The smack of his chest against the cement wall knocked the breath right out of him. The nerves in his injured leg screamed in protest.

His muscles burned and armpits ached from the weight of his legs dragging him down, but he pushed the pain out of his mind. He had to lift his body onto the ledge before his strength gave out, which he feared would be any second. Shuffling and pulling, he threw his leg onto the flat area above him and then pushed up with his knee. It took a few seconds, but he finally landed on his stomach in the opening.

Rather than get up, he rolled to his back and gasped for breath in the middle of what turned out to be an oversize air duct. Lying there, he could hear the mumble of voices below. He had no idea if they looked up or if they could see any part of his suit or body sticking out.

His brain slowly started working again. It

was only then he heard Maura's wild screams in his ear.

"Answer me!"

"I'm fine." The gruff whisper sounded strange to his ears. He had to admit he didn't sound fine. Winded and out of gas, yes.

He still had to get out of the building.

He saw the number painted on the wall. "Give me the closest and least public route out."

"I can only see the greasy ceiling, so get up."

Liam eased up, ignoring his creaking bones as he went. Every part of him from his fingers to his lower back to his leg ached. He felt every single one of his thirty-two years. For the first time since he left the force, he thought it was a good thing he no longer worked undercover. A man could only punish his body for so long before it gave out. He wasn't ready for that outcome and didn't want to make choices that sped up the process.

"Crawl to your left until I tell you to stop." Her voice boomed through the earpiece from out of nowhere.

It sure as hell woke him up. Without question, he followed her directions. He took every turn she said to take and stayed in control when his mind tried to wander to the building search that was likely being conducted for him right now. Exactly three minutes later, he popped out in a closet and knocked his head into a janitor's cart.

She laughed. "Nice move."

"You try being a superhero and see how you do."

"You're very manly."

"That's more like it." He opened the door a crack and peeked out. "Where from here?"

"Go right to the end of the hall, down one flight of stairs to the emergency door. At that point, you're underground but outside, so run up a few flights and I'll come get you."

"Sounds easy." He studied the entire area looking for signs of life. "That would be a nice change."

"The alarm will sound, but who cares. You can't risk walking back through that lobby."

"True."

He conducted one last scan of the area. Two people came around the corner. They were the first signs of life he'd seen since the lobby. When they disappeared into a set of double doors halfway down the white hallway, he went for it.

He didn't try to hide the sound of his shoes hitting the metal stairs. Neither did the group of men clomping up toward him.

"He's there," one said.

"Lock it down," another yelled.

Liam ignored their disconnected orders and the possibility of being caught. Running now, he flew down the stairs, only touching the railings as a way to help him take flight and skip more steps. He saw the door just as two guards hit the landing below him.

"Stop!"

No way was he listening to that. He pushed against the emergency bar and braced for the squeal of the high-pitched alarm. For some reason, the sound never came. Only the shouts of the guards followed him.

Rather than question his luck at pulling away, Liam sprinted out into the light. He looked around for an easy place to hide.

"Maura?"

She didn't respond to him through the microphone. Now that he thought about it, she hadn't said anything for a few minutes. When the SUV they'd rented pulled right up beside him and slammed on the brakes, he knew why.

She pushed open the passenger door. "Get in."

DAN LINDSEY BROKE THE YELLOW police tape and used his key to access his sister's apartment. Two steps in, his heart stopped. The place looked a lot like a bomb went off in here, too.

"Maura?" He knew calling for her was a waste of breath, but he had to try.

She had been missing ever since her lab went up in flames. In those initial hours, he grieved the loss of his baby sister, the only family left in his life. They'd lost their parents five years before in a car crash. The pain still lingered, hit him from nowhere now and then, but didn't live in him every day as it once had.

Learning he'd lost Maura under equally shocking circumstances drove him to his knees. He ran a computer business and teamed up with Liam on projects now and then. He wasn't the type to wallow or break down, but when the police delivered the news, he lost it.

After a day in an alcohol-fueled stupor with only Liam to keep him from jumping off a balcony, Dan sobered up in time for a second shock. The police insisted Maura was alive and on the run. Then Detective Spanner implicated Liam in the mess. To keep his mind from racing from one tragic ending to another, Dan needed to track Maura down.

He walked into the kitchen, turned over broken furniture and kicked the clothes aside. He saw a mess. He didn't discover one clue about Maura's whereabouts. Twenty minutes later, he stood in the middle of her apartment and glanced around one last time. Everything was out of place but nothing stuck out. He swore under his breath as he grabbed his keys off the breakfast bar.

Next stop, Liam's house.

Dan opened the door to the hallway. He didn't see the man or the gun until it was too late.

Chapter Nine

Rex Smithfield walked into the lab for the second time in two days. Dr. Hammer hated being disturbed almost as much as he despised Smithfield and his never-ending supply of expensive dark suits.

"Is there a problem?" Dr. Hammer didn't pretend to be busy doing something else. That strategy never worked because when Smithfield walked in, he demanded full attention.

"Why would there be?"

"You're here again. I figure you have better things to do."

Smithfield's eyebrow lifted in a rare show of emotion. "I am protecting my investment."

The calculations started in Dr. Hammer's head. The only way to rein in his temper over Smithfield's attitude was to visualize the many ways he could kill the man before the guards could get in there to save him. Several regular lab chemicals would stop his heart.

"I can't work with disruptions," Dr. Hammer said.

"Since I own this building and your time, you will do whatever I tell you to do." Smithfield's voice hit like a sharp slap.

"That wasn't the deal."

"You faked your own kidnapping in order to get out from under the restrictions of your NIH contract and earn much more money. I would not think a man in that position, someone who would sell out his professional ethics, would be all that concerned about contract provisions."

"My priority is my research."

"I will let you reason all that out. I am here for another purpose."

"Which is?"

"I may need your services for a project this evening."

The turn in the conversation left Dr. Hammer speechless. One minute Smithfield unleashed his icy wrath, the next he talked business.

"It would appear Dr. Lindsey and her washed-up policeman are planning a break-in to the building. I assume you are the target. You and this lab."

Dr. Hammer's heart thudded with enough force to break out of his chest. "She can't know about my work here."

"Clearly, she does."

Dr. Hammer tried to match what he knew about Maura to the vigilante woman Smithfield described. "None of this sounds like her. She's not the type to get involved with nonsense. She worked, slept and then worked again. That's it."

"I find that people under pressure do not always act how we expect them to."

"But why would she come here?"

Smithfield took time to inspect his manicured fingernails. "As I suspected, she figured out your tie to me."

"And she's bringing the police?" Dr. Hammer's mouth went dry. He was not the type to panic, but the thought of having his plan uncovered and the resulting loss of respect in the community filled him with a thudding dread. If his heart didn't slow its tick, he might fall down.

But he couldn't let Smithfield see any weakness. The man thrived on instilling anxiety and fear in others. Reveled in it.

"I doubt your Dr. Lindsey will go anywhere but here. As of this afternoon, the evidence surrounding the explosion will point only to her, a disgruntled employee who saw herself as better than she was. She needed to be the star and could not abide being forced to act the role of assistant." Smithfield shrugged as if destroying a young woman's life meant nothing. "It happens all the time in business."

The plan proved how much Smithfield still underestimated Maura. Dr. Hammer vowed not to make that mistake. "It is hard to imagine her rushing in here and demanding answers."

"Yes. A risky move for an otherwise intelligent woman."

Dr. Hammer pushed aside thoughts of Maura. He had to save his work. Someone else would have to rescue her. "There's no way for her to enter the building without you knowing."

"I suspect she will cause a diversion of some sort. Frankly, if she has trouble breaching the exterior, I will help her in."

"Why would you do that?" The shocked

question escaped before Dr. Hammer could censor it.

The displeasure showed on the harsh lines of Smithfield's face. "That is not your concern."

"What do you want me to do?"

"Be ready."

"I don't understand."

"When I need you, I will let you know."

MAURA STOOD IN A PARKING LOT a few hours later and watched Liam get ready. She didn't argue with his plan except for the timing. Going that night meant short preparation. She trusted him, but she also trusted her instincts and ability to reason. If she had more time, she'd sit down and look at the variables.

There was something in Smithfield Enterprises worth hiding. She bet the "something" in question was five foot nine and wore a lab coat. For a genius, Dr. Hammer seemed to have stumbled into something pretty stupid.

"My guy is handling the logistics of making the call look real," Liam said as he pulled his belt through the hoops and clipped it at his trim waist.

"You have interesting friends."

"This one owes me a favor." Liam slipped the navy long-sleeve shirt on over his tee.

The glimpse of broad chest and long fingers gave her comfort. "You sure your man can fool the right people into thinking this call is coming from inside the building?"

"Dummy phone and a router. We're covered." He buttoned up the shirt.

"Sounds like it."

"We go in with the emergency responders in the late afternoon and then wait it out in the catering kitchen until after hours. Once the place clears out, we'll have more freedom to move around."

"How are we going to get into the individual offices and the labs? This place seems to be in permanent lockdown."

"I haven't figured that part out yet."

That wasn't the response she expected. "Believe it or not, I don't find that very comforting."

He grabbed the keys off the hood of the ambulance. "You really want to panic? We can talk about the problems with disabling the cameras, getting by the guards and dodging whatever other nasty security measures this Smithfield guy has in place."

"Almost makes me wish the explosion had worked and taken me out of this mess."

Liam stopped fidgeting. "Don't joke about that."

The flat line of his mouth let her know how serious he was. He went from focused on the job to furious with her in two seconds.

She held up her hands in surrender. "You're right. Not funny."

Despite all the trauma and exhaustion, she had to smile at his EMT badge and official patches on his sleeves. If he ever left the security business, he could switch careers to EMT in a second. The uniform sure looked good on him. Everything did.

"Why are you staring at me?" he asked as he fiddled with his belt buckle. Didn't even glance up this time.

"I bet you were a great police officer."

"Not really."

His denial killed her brief moment without panic about what was ahead of them. "What does that mean?"

"You read the paper."

The media painted him as the villain, a cop out of control. She couldn't believe he would put an innocent at risk as everyone reported, or that he picked capturing a drug dealer over protecting a victim. Careless and unfeeling? Not the man who set his entire life aside to help her and attacked a police officer just to keep her safe.

Since she didn't know what else to say, she said the obvious. "That wasn't your fault."

"A woman died. I have to own that."

"You know there's more to the story."

Liam walked around to the driver's side of the truck. "We're done with this discussion."

In the past, when anyone used that tone or ignored her, she retreated. The intellectual world promised an escape from everything mean and bad. Lost in her books and studies, she didn't think about how she'd lost her parents, didn't worry that she'd never be normal. She could look the way she wanted and limit her interaction to slides and cells and paperwork. She didn't have to worry about being young or awkward. Her mind could race and her words could run together and no one judged.

Being with Liam the last few days she learned something else. Sharing the burden eased her frustration.

"It's okay to be a hero," she said.

"That's not what this is about."

She followed him, boxed him in when he tried to open the truck door. The move forced him to choose between shoving her away and facing her. To her relief, he went with standing there, arms hanging at his sides, an annoyed frown on his lips.

"Tell me what really happened that day." She stood close enough to touch him but refrained.

He wrapped his fingers around her forearms as if he wanted to move her. The hold never tightened. "We have work to do."

To stop him from pushing this aside and shutting her out of whatever was happening in his head, she rested her palm against his chest. His heart thumped against her hand. "Tell me."

"I'd rather kiss you."

Tall and dark, this man screamed temptation. "You're avoiding the conversation."

"Yes."

Her hand caressed his chest, rolling over the firm muscles and dipping into the sleek smoothness of his stomach. "Not even going to deny your subterfuge?"

"Not my style." He smiled then. "But if you

keep doing that with your fingers I'm definitely going to follow through on that kiss."

Her other hand joined the first.

Heat flared behind his green eyes. "One kiss and then back to work."

"I'm not stopping you." She wanted the press of his mouth against hers more than she wanted anything in that moment.

When his lips touched hers, all thoughts of digging into his past and picking at the psychology behind his decision to leave the police force disappeared. All that mattered was the woodsy smell of his skin and the firm grasp of his hands against the small of her back.

His mouth moved over hers, sending a signal to her arms to wrap around his neck. His tongue slipped against her teeth as the sound of his deep breaths played in her ears. It was a slow seduction of hands and mouth. It wiped out her common sense.

For the first time in her life, her mind shut off and her heart took over. She let the lightness pour through her without examining it. It tortured her when he broke off the kiss, but the gentle nuzzling of his nose against her cheek soothed her.

He leaned his forehead against hers. "I've been wanting to do that since our last kiss."

"Why didn't you?"

"You weren't into it."

She pulled her head back to stare up at him. "How can you say that?"

"Ah, let's see. I was planning on how to get under the covers with you and you were reviewing Hammer's documents in your head and pulled out the Smithfield name instead of saying mine."

She didn't know what he was talking about. "I never told you to stop."

At six-foot, he stood about five inches taller than her. The difference made her feel safe and protected. Despite all she'd accomplished, there was something comforting in knowing she didn't need to have all the answers or do all the work. She could depend on Liam for help. Sharing the burden usually made her feel weak. This time it empowered her.

His thumb traced the outline of her lips. "Maybe you didn't call it off with this mouth, but you did with your eyes. With your head."

"I don't know what that means."

"The insecurity peeks through whenever you leave the intellectual stuff and venture into emotional territory." He brushed her hair back, letting his fingers linger over her cheek. "A certain sadness moves over you when you can't rely on your smarts as a crutch."

If he had used anything but a soft and caring voice, she would have been offended. Would have insisted, as she always did, that she couldn't separate the smart part of her from the rest and people just had to accept that.

Instead, she went with the first words to strike her consciousness. "I'm most comfortable in the lab."

"But you're a woman wherever you go. You have needs and desires. I know because I've felt them."

The doubt backed up on her out of nowhere. She was transported back to a time when he'd turned her away.

She dropped her hands and stepped back. "We should get going."

Nice and slow he brought her body back to his, let her feel every muscle and bulge. "How long before you forgive me for the past?"

"I did the second you tackled that guy on your deck and threatened the detective."

"I don't think so."

But she did. The memory from all those

years ago still stung. It fueled her, shaped who she was and how she structured her life to erase every ounce of the teenager inside her from there forward. As much as she wanted to blame him, those choices were hers. She'd carried them and wallowed in them for years, but she was old enough to move on now.

"I wouldn't be standing with you now if I hated you for something that happened when I was a kid," she said.

"But you're still hiding behind your big brain."

"That's the part nobody gets. It's a package deal."

"But it doesn't have to erase the woman inside."

"I don't know what you mean."

"Not yet, but you will."

She wasn't sure how they got there or where they were. "Does this have something to do with your shooting?"

"No."

"I don't—"

He placed a short, hard kiss on her lips. "It's time to go."

Chapter Ten

The piercing fire-truck whistle drowned out most of the shouting. Two burly security guards held open the huge glass doors leading to Smithfield Enterprises. Men in business suits scrambled out of the way as ambulance crews piled into the lobby. People pointed and questioned each other about what was happening.

It was controlled chaos.

The guard in the middle of the frenzy of people and drowning noise directed the emergency crews to the elevator banks. Gurneys rolled across the pristine marble floor.

"Which floor?" a paramedic asked.

A guard slipped an arm into the car and turned the key. "Go up to the tenth."

Through all the confusion, one EMT stepped up and demanded access to another elevator for faster access. The guard with the key complied. Just as he had been ordered to do.

Rex Smithfield leaned back in his oversize leather desk chair and took in the scene on one of the six security monitors sitting in front of him. On another, he watched Dr. Hammer shuffle around his lab, oblivious to the camera aimed right at his head or the plan hatching just a few floors below him.

The two supposed medical professionals in the second elevator matched the file photos of Dr. Lindsey and her boyfriend in body type. The way they hid their faces confirmed it. The man's finger hovered over the button for the fifth floor until he spared a brief glance at the camera on the car's ceiling. He hit ten instead.

Smithfield studied the couple. They carried duffel bags and never spoke to each other. Nothing in their movements suggested desperation to get to an injured employee. The careening rush of the lobby had disappeared. They acted as though they planned to stay for a long time.

It appeared that Maura Lindsey and Liam

Anderson believed they were in control of the situation.

They would learn.

THE ENTRY WENT ACCORDING to plan. The execution, the hiding, all of it worked.

Liam knew something was wrong.

They should have met resistance, at least had to duck for cover somewhere along the line. Instead, they spent the last three hours hanging out in the abandoned catering kitchen. The room's one camera stayed stationary. All they had to do was stay out of the center of the room and wait out the employees as they cleared out for home.

Yeah, too damn easy.

Maura sat on the metal prep table, swinging her legs back and forth and staring at the gun next to her. "I wish I knew how to shoot."

"Just aim and pull the trigger. The only rule is that you don't shoot me."

"You're on edge."

He was sneaking around a high-security building with a novice and a plan with a very low probability of working. He'd be happy to just be on edge. "I'm fine."

"You sound stressed."

"Only an idiot would be calm right now."

He weighed telling her the extent of his concern. Dressed in her fake ambulance crew uniform with her hair in a ponytail and nibbling on her bottom lip, she looked vulnerable. Then his gaze went to her eyes. Fueled with anger over her boss's dishonesty, this woman was ready for battle. That realization cooled the flare of his protective instincts.

He'd throw his body in front of hers, do whatever had to be done to track down the information to clear her name, but he wouldn't get stuck calming a crying woman. She was not the type.

Despite being at an age when most of her peers still viewed weekends as prime drinking time, Maura thrived on responsibility. Probably too much so. She didn't whither under pressure. Didn't dig a hole and avoid danger. She rushed in, rage burning, when something mattered to her.

Not that she understood her strength. She measured her life only in terms of intellectual pursuits and tried to convince others to do the same. Escaping from a burning building and tracking down a rogue doctor spoke to her inner toughness. It showed him she possessed much more than a lab coat and a beautiful face. How to convince her of that was the question.

"If you clench your hand any tighter you're going to break a bone."

He followed her gaze to his hard fist. It took an effort for him to ease up on his grip. "I guess I'm not used to busting into office buildings."

She shrugged. "We aren't stealing information or anything like that."

"We're still committing a felony. Believe it or not, that's not how I usually spend my evenings."

She burst out laughing. When the sound bounced off the shiny surfaces and grew louder, she put her hand over her mouth as if to call it back.

He couldn't imagine what she found funny about their current situation. Having the police and a Smithfield goon squad after them kept his heart thudding at an uncontrollable pace. "What?"

"You look a little green, as if you just realized how far you've strayed from your law-enforcement ways since I dropped on your back deck."

"Trouble does follow you."

"It never did before."

He loaded the last of the building schematics from his small notebook computer to the two dummy phones. "Thanks to the Smithfield tech team, we'll be able to move around with some sense of where we are. We can see a blueprint of the rooms and exits."

She caught the phone when he threw it. "What about the security cameras and alarmed locks on every door?"

"You aren't thinking positively."

"Sure I am or I would have mentioned the guards crawling all over this place." She managed to smile as she said it.

"The cameras are going to blink."

Her mouth went flat. "Excuse me?"

He held up a small black box. It fit into the palm of his hand and could cause more damage than the gun tucked into his waistband. "Electromagnetic pulse."

"Seriously?"

"Don't worry. It's the non-nuclear kind."

She jumped down and stood in front of him with her fingers resting on the device. "You're going to disable the cameras with this thing?"

"That's the plan."

Her eyes brightened at the thought. Liam could see the scientist in her getting excited. Energy vibrated around her as she turned the piece over and studied it with open-mouthed appreciation. "This is fascinating."

He felt pride surge through him. "It's a high-intensity short burst that will knock out any electronics that are on at the time of the shot. Our phones and my computer will stay off until after we deliver the pulse. That should keep us up and running after the meltdown."

"But it will disable their fancy alarm and camera system." She flashed him a wide smile. "That's brilliant."

"From what I can tell, Smithfield has a backup system. We'll only have a short window to get in and find what we need, and that's only if Smithfield hasn't figured out a way to make his electronics EMP resistant."

She smoothed her fingers over the plastic box with a reverence other people used on religious icons. "I don't pretend to be an expert in physics, but you'd normally need a generator and an antenna for optimal coupling."

He knew the term had to do with transferring power but his knowledge of the specifics ended there. "Only if you intend a significant and sustained attack. I'm not talking about launching a missile in here. This is for a much more concentrated purpose."

She stopped turning it over and investigating. "How did you get this? This has to be top-secret military equipment."

"The technology has been around for decades."

Her eyebrow inched up. "That's not really an answer."

"I'm a security expert, remember? I have all sorts of secrets and friends in very low places." The gadget was just one of the many he used to do his work. Every tool gave him an advantage. People hired him, trusted him, for a reason. He didn't shrink away from doing the difficult thing, even if that meant walking right up to the line of legality.

She nodded. "I'm ready."

He debated leaving her in this room for the hundredth time. She had proven she could handle a tough situation. Still, the idea of anything happening to her made his stomach spin.

"Don't even think about it," she said in a deadpan voice.

"What?"

"This is my life. My mess. You are not tying me to a chair or whatever."

"That would be extreme, don't you think?"

"You need me for the Dr. Hammer piece. You don't know what you're looking for." She held up a palm. "And before you start thinking I'm calling you dumb, all I'm saying is that I'm not sure what we're looking for. I don't know what my dear boss is doing or why. I probably won't until I see him and get a look at whatever is happening here."

"This is dangerous."

"So is prison and we both know that's where I'm heading if we fail here." She dropped a quick kiss on Liam's mouth before stepping back again. "We're in this together."

"You'll follow my lead?"

"Of course."

Her quick answer didn't give him any comfort. He picked up her hand and lifted it to his lips. "If you get a shot to get out of here with whatever you need to clear your name, you take it."

"Understood."

He kissed her knuckles. "Even if it means you leave me behind."

A shiver moved through her. He felt it under his lips. Saw her body jerk in reaction to his rough words.

Ever since branching out on his own, he had taken huge risks to finish the job, including putting his body on the line to rescue corporate kidnapping victims outside the United States. He'd gotten a reputation for sacrificing his personal safety for the job. People joked that he acted as if he didn't care what happened to him. Looking back on the suicide missions now, he wondered where his head had been. Loving the work was one thing. Sacrificing his life was another, and he often teetered on the line between.

When he looked at Maura, his priorities shifted. Saving her, getting her out of Hammer's disaster and helping her see that life existed outside of the lab gave him a purpose. He didn't know where they went from here or how they would ever get there, but he wanted her safe.

"Maura?"

"We are both going in and both coming out."

He kissed the inside of her wrist. "Promise me."

She hesitated. Seconds ticked by with her staring at him. He stared right back. This issue was too important to drop.

"Fine," she finally ground out between clenched teeth.

The tightening crank in his chest loosened. He needed all of his concentration to make this work, and that couldn't happen if he had to worry about her trying to rescue him. Sure, he'd only clued her in to half of his plan. Their exit strategy depended on Detective Spanner, but Maura didn't know that. Liam needed her focused on rescuing herself no matter what.

Liam gave her fingers a squeeze before dropping her hand. "Turn off your phone, pick up your gun and let's get started."

Without another word, they moved to either side of the doorway leading to the hallway. When he nodded to her, she performed a final check on her phone then gave him the all-clear signal. As the countdown sounded in his head, he mentally cataloged all the things that could go wrong in the next ten minutes. Then he saw her shoulders tense and eyes close as if waiting for an actual bomb to go off, and he hit the button.

A ripple went through him right before the lights blinked off. The whirring sounds of the building's electricity stopped and a deadly silence fell over the floor. The darkness inside now matched the black night outside the window. Someone on the street or in a neighboring building would soon notice and the guards, plus any remaining workers, had to be scrambling.

They didn't have any time to waste.

He turned on the flashlight mounting on his gun. The small beam of light would guide them until the auxiliary power kicked on or someone came hunting them.

"Let's go." Liam whispered the command as they slipped out into the dark corridor.

He listened for shouts or footsteps but nothing echoed back to him. The soundproofing between floors would make it tough to sense the enemy until they pounced. The worst trap would be the stairwells, and that was exactly where he needed to take Maura.

She walked with her back plastered against the wall. The gun waved around in front of her until he reached over and steadied it.

"I'm nervous," she said almost as an apology.

"It's just your body giving you the energy you need to get through this."

"Then why am I having trouble keeping my teeth from chattering and my knees from turning to mush?"

"Because you're human." He kept up the quiet conversation until they reached the end of the hall. The goal was to distract her while they moved and keep him from calling a halt to this insanity by smuggling her out of there.

When they reached the emergency door, he pressed against the handle with controlled pressure, hoping to keep the noise to a minimum. Didn't work. In the stillness, the click sounded like he hit the door with a sledgehammer.

Maura winced. "Easy."

"I'm trying."

He hung back, waiting to see if anyone jumped out or bullets flew before pushing forward. When quiet greeted him, he peeked inside the doorway. Nothing. No footsteps above or below him. He'd kill for night goggles and heat sensors right now, but the advanced equipment was locked away in his secret safe in his house. He'd only taken what was in reach when he tied up Spanner and left the house. Anything in the safe stayed there for fear of tipping Spanner off to its location.

That meant Liam had to rely on his ears and intuition. He tried to wash his mind clear of anything but focusing on the sights and sounds around him.

They started up the stairs, constantly looking around. He wanted to present a moving target if anyone came running after them. He also stayed on alert, ready to jump in front of Maura if needed. Ready to hit the emergency button and bring Spanner running if everything else failed.

Partway up, the lights flickered back on. Not the bright white flood. No, this was a dim blue glow that came from round fixtures in the corners.

When Maura frowned at him, he filled her in. "Secondary power."

"The electricity should be out."

"It is. This is a fallback system run through the generator." He picked that possibility up from the tech's system. Seemed the Smithfield folks didn't trust the security system to remain up and running no matter what."

"These guys thought of everything."

That was his fear. "Let's hope not."

Stairs thudded beneath his feet as two flights passed without resistance. The stairwell was clear. The only potential threat came from the strange metal lockers on each landing. They looked like walled-in phone booths but when he opened the door, all he saw was a series of cables and a slim shaft that led from the floor to the ceiling. If he had more time to explore, he'd check it out as a potential escape route. Not that he'd fit inside without curling into a ball. The space would never work.

A third flight passed and the silence remained. By the time they hit the landing right below the fifth floor, Liam was convinced they were walking into a trap. No mission ran without snags. With the security devices around this place, this job should have been worse than most. The exact opposite proved true.

No building experiencing an electronic blackout stayed this quiet. Guards should be running the stairs and searching the halls. The fact he could storm up the steps easier now than when he tried to walk in the front door during business hours with a security badge on his belt told Liam what he needed to know.

Hammer, or whoever was pulling the strings on Hammer, remained one step ahead.

Liam motioned for Maura to hang back and then inhaled as deep as possible before he opened the door to the floor a fraction. From his limited view he saw an empty hallway. Nothing to the right or in front of him.

He glanced back to fill Maura in but she was gone. He blinked several times, tried to get a grip on the panic racing through him before it swallowed everything. Then the door in front of him flew out of his hand. His head snapped around right as the gun barrel pressed against his forehead.

"Make a move and you're dead," said the guard.

Liam recognized the voice from his run-in with security the first time he tried to enter the building. The guy had a huge head and even bigger biceps. This time he wore full tactical gear, which proved what Liam feared all along. They knew he was coming.

"Take it easy," he said. No need for the guy to get itchy and start shooting.

The guy grabbed Liam's gun. "Where's your girlfriend?"

That's what Liam wanted to know.

Chapter Eleven

Maura sensed the setup right as it sprang. She picked up on Liam's anxiety. Watched as he steeled his body for the blow that might come when he opened the fifth-floor door. The same shot he was willing to take for her.

No way was she letting him walk into danger without giving him a chance to get out again. As Liam broke the seal on the door, she tiptoed backward, heading for the electrical locker in the corner of the landing. The hiding place would give her an extra second to launch an attack if Liam needed help. In a foreign environment with only the unknown around them, she needed to grab any opportunity that came along.

Fast as she could and without making any noise, she slipped inside. Her sneakers balanced on the thin rim of metal that edged the otherwise open floor. One shift and she'd lose her footing. With nothing to stop her free fall but a few wires—and she didn't even know if they would hold her weight—dropping into the hole beneath her would mean plummeting down into darkness. She refused to let that happen.

Stiff cables dug into her back and her shoulders curled in as she tried to make her body as small as possible. This was just one more time when she wished she were a petite scrap of a thing. Instead, she had hips and broad shoulders. It would be the ultimate punishment if her body type caused her death.

Tight and folded, she still took up every available inch of the box. The space made the car trunk seem roomy. Warm air blew up from underneath her but she still struggled to breathe. Rather than panic, she focused all of her energy on the weapon in her hand.

When the door whipped open without warning, she aimed the stun gun at her attacker. At the sizzling zap of the prongs, the big man's eyes popped wide. She didn't ease up on the contact after the first shot. She knew better. Three seconds and he'd be writhing in pain on the ground. If she could hold on even longer, then all the better.

Time sped by until she lost any sense of just how much had passed. The man dropped his gun, sending it bouncing against the steps as he flopped first to his knees and then into the fetal position.

With his body on the floor, she could see the guard behind him. He stood in the doorway with a gun aimed at Liam's head. As the scene unfolded, the man's body went lax. It was as if his muscles strained to fathom the sight of a woman taking out a two-hundred-and-twenty-plus-pound bruiser.

Liam didn't suffer from the same hesitation. He smashed his elbow up and into the guard's nose, snapping the man's head back and causing the hand with the gun to waver as the other one went to protect his face. Taking advantage of being free, Liam drove his shoulder into the guy's stomach, pressing him back into the far wall. Already off balance, the guard lost his footing and his gun went flying.

Liam had the weapon in his possession before the man slumped to the floor. A hit across the temple with the end of the gun knocked the man unconscious.

The sight of a bloody nose and cut on the head froze Maura for a second. She watched as Liam searched the man's pockets and removed his earpiece. Heard her victim roll around at her feet, moaning. She tried to take it all in and get her body going, but she just stood there unable to move for fear her heart would hammer right through her skin.

Liam glanced at her over his shoulder. "Come out of there."

His abrupt order got her moving. It also sent a wave of fury coursing through her veins. "You're welcome."

A pair of handcuffs appeared out of nowhere. "Nice work."

If he thought that would ease her jumbled thoughts or shaking fingers, he was wrong. "You have your strategy and I have mine."

"Speaking of that, where did the stun gun come from?"

"Years of living alone."

The weapon Liam gave her sat snugly against the small of her back. She had no idea how to shoot that one without injuring herself. She did know how to drop a man two times her size by sending a load of high voltage streaming through him. Aim first, apologize later if necessary. That was the motto of her self-defense instructor and she had followed it.

She lifted her leg to step over her attacker. Just as her front foot hit the floor, the man grabbed her other ankle in midair. With a twist, he wrenched her leg. Hard. Pain shot up her knee as he tugged her toward the floor.

"Liam!" She forced the word out.

Her stomach lodged in her throat as her upper body flew without stopping toward the cement floor. She braced for the whack, brought her hands up to lessen the impact.

But it never came. Liam reached out. His strong arm caught her under the arm. She let out a yelp of surprise to match his grunt. As one arm wrapped around her, the other lifted near her ear. She heard the click and soft plug right before the grip on her ankle dropped.

Liam dragged her away and into his arms. His hands traveled over her face and across her shoulders as if checking for broken bones and gunshots. "Are you okay?"

"Not really."

"Did he touch you?"

"What happened?" She glanced down into the open-eyed dead stare of the man who terrified her not two seconds before. The bullet hole in his forehead told her all she needed to know. The man couldn't hurt her now.

Liam gave her a little shake, one that forced her stunned eyes back to his face. "Maura, answer me."

She could barely speak. She moved her mouth but only a whimpering sound escaped. Sure, she'd seen corpses in school. She'd just never watched a life end. Not like this.

"You shot him," she said as the reality of their actions settled over her. Thanks to Dr. Hammer and the disaster he unleashed, two men were dead. Tom and this guy. She worried the death toll would keep rising.

Lines of stress appeared around Liam's mouth. "I had to do it. I didn't know what other weapons he might have, and couldn't risk letting him grab you, throw you down the stairs, anything."

Between the pale skin and strain stretching every inch of his face, Liam looked like someone had kicked him in the head. Stunned and desperate, he was trying to convince her that he wasn't a cold-blooded killer. As if that thought ever entered her mind.

She blew out the breath caught in her chest. "Thank you."

His shoulders fell back to normal height. "Really?"

"I don't think he planned to shake my hand."

"Well, yeah. I mean, I'm sorry you had to see that, but—"

She brushed the backs of her hands against Liam's cheek. "Ever the hero."

Those green eyes narrowed into slits. "What?"

"Never apologize for rescuing a woman from the bad guys."

The tension around his mouth lessened. "We're only alive at this moment because of you."

She did do that. Used more than her brains to get out of a situation. It was a new sensation and not an unwelcome one. "That's true."

"You were pretty impressive for a brainiac lab rat."

"I have skills."

"I just never expected one of them to be lethal self-defense moves." He bent down and searched the dead guy, uncovering a second gun and two knives. "I'm grateful, believe me."

"Happy to help out." She blew on the top of her stun gun, showing a moment of bravado she didn't feel. Her internal organs had turned to jelly. She doubted she'd ever be able to walk up a staircase without a bodyguard and her trusty stun gun again.

Liam treated her to one of his sexy smiles. "Let's go before their friends come looking for them."

But that was easier to say than to do. There was exactly one room on the floor, or that's what she figured from the huge steel door at the far end. A special suite suggested a special guest, one Maura supposed had more protection somewhere inside.

Liam nodded at the bubble on the ceiling. "The cameras are still out. The secondary power source must only cover the auxiliary lighting, but it could cycle and switch some other electronics on. I'd like to be gone if it does."

"No argument there."

Liam slipped something into his ear. "This should help."

"What is it?"

"The guard's microphone."

"Hear anything?"

Liam frowned. "No."

"Isn't that odd?"

"Isn't everything about Smithfield Enterprises strange?" He dragged the unconscious guard into the stairwell and stepped over him, closing the door behind him.

"The guy will wake up eventually and cause trouble."

"That's true." Liam jammed a small piece of black plastic under the door handle. "This will make it harder for anyone to get on this floor through this entrance."

"What if we need to use it to get out?"

"There's another exit. No way would the person who designed this jail disguised as an office building only leave one way off a floor. Too dangerous."

"Then let's go find Dr. Hammer and drag the weasel out of here."

"Exactly my thought."

They made their way to the door. The dark pad of the retinal scanner next to the door reminded her of the disabled security at the lab. The defenses went down right before the place blew up. She hoped they weren't in for a second round of fireballs.

"You think there are more guards in there?" she asked, more to burn off some of the energy bouncing around inside her than to actually get an answer. She knew the answer.

He tapped on the guard's earpiece before putting it back in again. "Don't you?"

"Yes."

Liam tried the door but it didn't budge.

"Is it still locked?" she asked.

"Probably just another level of security. Some extra bar that slides shut when the electricity goes off."

"So, now what?"

"We blow it, of course." He took a packet out of his front pants pocket. Unwrapping the white paper, he uncovered a ball of putty.

"I'm guessing that's explosive material." She didn't need a degree to recognize it.

He dropped to his knees and smoothed a small glob of the substance over the lock keypad. The phone came next. After some fiddling, he removed a small stick from the side and plunged it into the putty.

Once he set the device, he glanced up at her. "We need to get to the other end of the hall."

The scientist inside her wanted to investigate the mechanism and understand exactly how it worked. The rest of her, the parts that wanted to live through the next few minutes, didn't argue. "Okay."

They hustled to the other end of the corridor. With his finger over a button on the back of his phone, he hesitated. "You shoot at anything that comes out of that room."

"I got it."

"No stun guns this time. Actual bullets."

She could barely hear him over the thunder of blood as it rushed to her ears. "I don't plan on dying in the middle of the fifth floor of Smithfield Enterprises or going down for Dr. Hammer's kidnapping, so anything that moves gets hit."

"That's the spirit." His finger hovered for one more second. "Ready?"

His directions and bossiness were making her nuts. "Push the darn thing."

A smile tugged at the corner of Liam's mouth right before he pressed down. "Yes, ma'am."

The screeching boom blew the lock inside the room and shook the floor beneath them. Puffs of smoke rolled down the hallway toward them. Glass crashed and metal crunched. Dust fell from the drywall around the doorjamb.

She coughed as the particle-filled air reached them. "You're very good at your job."

"Let's hope that continues."

Before she could answer, Liam jogged toward the busted door. He stood with his back to the wall and crouched down to look inside, standing up only long enough to motion her closer. As she reached him, he slipped his arm inside the hole.

"What are you doing?" she asked in a harsh whisper.

"Getting us in there."

The lock clicked and the door swung open. After everything it took to get there, she feared taking one more step. "I'm not sure we're safer in there."

"Me, either, but that bolt I stuck in the stairway door is only going to hold it shut for a short time. We keep moving forward or…"

"Yeah, I get it."

She expected to walk into an expensive lab. She stepped into a windowless living room. The small room had a couch and chair. Not a piece of equipment in sight. "What the heck is this?"

"I have no idea." He put a hand on her shoulder. "Stay here."

She ignored the order and followed him with her hand wrapped in the back of his shirt. "I'd rather stick with you."

"Apparently."

Liam led with his gun as he walked into the kitchen area and the small bathroom next to it. A space off to the side hid a double bed. Spare furniture. No obvious places to hide. No closets. Only a rack of clothes and lab coats and a few piled boxes next to the bed.

The layout didn't make any sense to her. "It's an apartment in the middle of a floor of an office building."

"It's internal. I don't see a window or any access to light."

"It's like a cell."

"It doesn't take up the entire floor, so there's something else up here. We just have to figure out how to get to it." Liam smoothed his hand over the walls as if looking for a secret entrance.

"I'm still trying to figure out why this is here. It's so out of context."

"It gives Hammer somewhere to live while he works."

She spun around in a circle, taking in every inch of the makeshift studio. "He gave up his big house and trophy wife for this? I don't get it."

"Money."

"What?"

"This is a temporary situation. There must be a pot of cash in this for Hammer somewhere."

"He already earns good money. He has patents which bring in other income."

"He's earning government scientist money. I imagine his findings could be significantly more lucrative in the private sector."

"If that's true, where is he?"

A creaking by the front door had them both swinging. Liam's gun came up as fast as his head whipped around. Her instincts misfired. She stood there with her finger on the trigger and the muzzle pointed at her feet as if her mind refused to telegraph a different message to her hand.

She expected a rush of guards to storm through the opening. Instead, the hole went dark as something snapped shut in front of it. One minute she saw shadows in the hallway.

The next she stared at a seemingly solid door. "What just happened?"

"Someone locked us inside."

Chapter Twelve

"Has your sister always been a criminal or can we blame this on your friend, the scandal-prone police officer?" Rex Smithfield used the remote to stop the image, rewind and show it again.

Dan refused to answer. His mind still hadn't adjusted to seeing Maura alive. The first time she appeared on the screen his heart actually jumped. The heavy darkness of the last few days lifted. Or it did until he saw what this man was doing to her. Dan tried not to look at the monitor as pain raced across Maura's face and the door slammed shut, locking her inside the bizarre apartment-like area.

Dan didn't know where he was, where all of this action was unfolding, because he'd been unconscious when he arrived. But he did know that his sister and best friend were in huge trouble. The egotistical whack job pacing around in front of Dan was setting them up, luring them in and watching every move.

"What do you want?" Dan asked the question over the burning in his shoulder blades and the debilitating fear rumbling around in his stomach.

"What every businessman wants. To run his office in peace and without interference from meddling women."

The guy might think the expensive suit made him legitimate, but the ropes biting into Dan's wrists suggested something else. He twisted his hands behind his back to find a better position. With each tug, the bindings grew tighter. When moisture landed against his fingertips, he knew he had rubbed the skin raw and it had started bleeding.

"Let us go and you can do that," he suggested. "We don't care what's happening here. Hell, I don't even know who you are."

"Rex Smithfield."

Dan cultivated business contacts. He knew Smithfield by reputation. Divorced, reclusive and pathologically driven. He didn't mingle and insisted on the best of everything. As far as Dan could tell, the other man resembled many men of his position. He had an oversize ego and the bank account to match, but no scandals that jumped to mind.

"You're an honest businessman." Dan had no idea whether that was true, but he decided to go for the man's biggest asset—his overinflated sense of his self-worth. "You don't want to mess with this sort of thing."

"I'm afraid it is too late for that. You see, your sister got in my way."

"She did her job. That's all she ever does."

"Apparently not."

Dan ignored the comment and pressed ahead with the pleading. "She cares about her lab, not the business angles. Just let everyone go, let her get back to her research, and we can all move on."

Smithfield's cold laughter filled the small abandoned office. "I believe what she is *researching* is Mr. Anderson."

That was the third time Smithfield had referred to a relationship between Maura and Liam since Dan recovered from the crack to his head and woke up. Even now, he didn't believe it. If anything, Liam and Maura had always gone out of their way to avoid each other. The pseudo separation made Dan nuts.

Having the two people closest to him hate each other ruined most holiday get-togethers. He'd never understood except to assume their stark differences made them little more than tolerant of each other.

But now he saw something soft in Maura's eyes when she looked at Liam, the same feeling that was mirrored in the way Liam touched her. Either the circumstances drove them together or something else did.

"They actually make an interesting couple, don't you think?" Smithfield asked with a heavy dose of amusement in his voice as he froze the frame on their faces. "The bright young lab assistant and the dirty cop."

Dan's gaze flipped to the screen and then back to Smithfield's empty smile. "What does Liam have to do with any of this?"

Smithfield tapped the remote against his chin. "If I were you, I would question the cop's influence here. Did she break into buildings and set fires before she started sleeping with him? I bet not."

Dan blocked the man's deep voice from his mind. He refused to let the words seep in. Liam and Maura would get out of there safe and unharmed. There was no one in the world Dan trusted more with his sister's safety than Liam.

Smithfield stepped over and stood right in front of Dan's chair, forcing him to look up. "It's a shame, really."

"We're done talking."

"Your sister had so much potential. If I had realized how inventive she was, that she was not the mousy isolated creature Hammer insisted her to be, I might have talked to her about my plans, as well."

"She never would have listened to you." Dan had no idea what this man planned except that he wasn't above killing people to get what he wanted. No way would Maura get roped into that sort of mess voluntarily.

"I admit I find her attractive in a scientific experiment sort of way. A brilliant mind and curvy body are an interesting combination."

Dan kicked out, hoping to hurt this smug guy, but his feet were tied down. The chair teetered. He only avoided falling over by throwing his weight in the opposite direction.

Smithfield stepped back. "Settle down."

"If you touch her, I will kill you." In his furious haze Dan knew he could do it. If his hands were free, he'd wrap his fingers around this guy's neck and stop whatever madness he had planned.

"I am afraid she has already outlived her usefulness. The evidence for the lab explosion points to her, but I cannot have her around to contest it." Smithfield tilted his head to the side. "I am sure you understand."

Bile rushed up the back of Dan's throat. "Liam won't let that happen and he's too smart to let you catch him."

"Which is why you're here." Smithfield set the remote down on the television stand. "I think your friend will risk his life to save you, and that is when I will have him. So, really, I should thank you for snooping around your sister's house. You made it easy to hatch a new plan."

"WE HAVE TO FIND THE OTHER way out." Maura slid her hands over the plaster walls.

"We will." Liam sat down on the couch. He needed a second to think. He expected to fight off guards. He didn't anticipate a locked studio in the middle of an office building. His mind rebelled against the new facts.

She spared him a brief glance. "Get up and

help me. They could be planning anything and we're trapped."

That wasn't right. Something bigger was happening here. This was about more than taking a scientist and stealing his findings. This was a sick game of cat and mouse. Every time Liam got them to the next level, an unseen force pulled the strings and sent them careening in a new direction. Getting in the building, through security, away from the guards—it all unfolded at a pace and in a way to suggest someone else was controlling it. The entire evening had been a well-played trap.

He had to get Maura out of there.

"We should leave. Get down the stairs and out of the building. I can call Spanner from the street and convince him to get a warrant to search this place."

She shot him an are-you-crazy glare. "On what grounds? Without Dr. Hammer or the evidence, we have nothing."

Liam balanced his elbows on his knees and studied the floor. "We're still alive, which is more than I can say for that guard in the stairwell."

"We've come too far to turn around now."

"Don't you get it?" He shoved up from the cushions and stood there staring at her, willing her to understand and leave with him before she got hurt. Her life was too precious to risk in this way. "They, whoever *they* are, want us to find the other entrance and use it. We're just playing into someone else's twisted game."

She dropped her arms to her sides. "So, you're suggesting we sit here and wait for the guards to come for us? How is that a better option? At least if we go in shooting we have a chance of winning."

"Those odds aren't good enough for me."

"You can't tell me you've never fought through worse. I've heard the rumors, listened as Dan bragged about you. This can't be the hardest job of your life."

"This one is different."

"Why?"

He touched his fingers to his forehead. He hoped the right words would pop into his head, but nothing came. Rather than come up with a fancy sentence he said what he felt. "You."

The tension seeped out of her face and the strain over her eyes eased. "Liam."

"It's taken nine years to get you to talk to me without turning away or cutting me off."

Red splotches stained her cheeks. "This can't be about an incident when I was a teenager."

"It's about everything."

"You know what I think?" The embarrassment turned to anger. It sparked in her eyes and vibrated down to her clenched fists and stiff knees.

"What's wrong with you?"

She threw her hands out wide to her sides. "You and your secrecy. You and the blame you take on even when it isn't yours to wear."

The clicking sound was his brain shutting down. It happened every time anyone tiptoed into this topic. He saw it coming and avoided.

"Now isn't the right time for this conversation. You were right. We should keep looking for an exit." He tried to scoot around her but she grabbed his arm.

"You walked into a domestic dispute and tried to reason with an abusive jackass. You used all of your training and said what you were supposed to say. You played by the rules because that's what your supervisor told you to do, and the guy shot his wife anyway."

The words bounced right off him. "I know what happened. I was there."

Her fingers tightened on his arm. "It shook your confidence, maybe it even changed you, but you know what? You're a rescuer by nature. It's who you are no matter how much you try to bury it. Even now, even though you hate that part of you and it scares you, your instinct is to step in and protect me."

"I couldn't stand it if something happened to you."

"You can't lose confidence now. Don't you get it? If you spin out of control, I will follow along, and I can't afford to do that."

The trembling started in her hands and took over every muscle until he thought she'd split into a hundred pieces. The realization that he'd brought her to this, not Hammer or the situation, humbled him. He never would have guessed he had that power.

"Damn, I'm sorry." He massaged her arms, trying to warm her chilled skin.

"I can't do this alone."

"And you're not going to. We're going to calm down and figure this out."

"Are you kidding? I can barely breathe." She bent over and inhaled loud enough for him to hear the labored sound as if it were right near his ear. Her hair fell over her shoulders and her whole body shook.

It was as if all of her bones turned to mush, leaving her limp and almost lifeless. He rubbed her lower back, trying to soothe her with soft words and an even softer touch. "Hey, it's going to be fine."

She continued to gulp in large mouthfuls of air. "How can you say that?"

With her weakening, he had no choice but to be strong. "Have I been wrong so far?"

She peeked up through strands of silky brown hair. "You do understand we're stuck in here, right?"

"Stand up." He helped her do just that.

"I'm going to strangle Dr. Hammer if we find him."

"We will and you can't." When she started to argue, Liam rushed to explain. "Well, not until he tells Detective Spanner you're innocent."

"And if my idiot boss won't make that admission?"

"We'll take turns cutting off his air supply."

She finally smiled. "Look, I know we're walking into an ambush, but I can't sit here."

She was right. They'd figure out how best to

go through the hidden door once they actually found it.

"I'll check the kitchen." He turned to head into the small room at the far left end and stopped when he realized he was the only one moving.

Maura stood in the middle of the room with her hands on her hips.

"Taking a break already?" he asked.

"We're going about this the wrong way."

"We haven't really started."

"This is a doorway Dr. Hammer would use."

"Well, yeah."

"Despite the high I.Q., my boss is inept in many ways. He depends on his wife to usher him around for speaking engagements. He relied on me to keep the office running. Heck, he couldn't fix the copy machine if it got jammed."

"So?"

"The entrance is something simple, almost obvious."

Liam's mind went right to the only personal items in the entire place. "The bedroom."

They rushed to the side of the bed. Hangers squeaked against the metal rod as they shoved back the clothes and unstacked the boxes sitting on the floor. There, on the wall, was the faint outline of a door. The opening was so thin the door had to scrape against the frame when it opened. If Liam could find the knob he'd do just that.

"Push." Her voice barely registered above a whisper.

He understood the solution without her assistance. The point was to go in strong and not get killed. That meant keeping Maura back and heading in first. He pointed at her and then pointed in the corner.

She shook her head in response. The mutinous tight-lipped scowl told him her position. She didn't need the words. But that didn't mean he agreed. If he had to protect her and shoot at the same time, he'd do it.

When she held her ground, he gave in. Sort of. He motioned behind him, then shifted her hips until his body blocked as much of hers as possible. With his left hand raised, he counted down the seconds to entry. As the last finger fell, he slammed against the door with his shoulder. It flipped open with a loud scratching sound.

He entered gun up and yelling. Pointing in

every direction, he waited for someone—anyone—to jump out. He saw only shiny surfaces and equipment he didn't recognize. Notes littered the floor, and strings of data showed on every computer screen on a long desk that seemed to function as a workstation.

"This definitely is the lab," Maura said as she stepped around him.

He threw out his arm to keep her back. "Not yet."

"There's no one here."

"Just hang back for a second."

This time she listened and stayed still when he moved forward. The computers held her attention. She paged through notes and walked her finger down the screen.

He pointed his gun at the far end of the room. The huge doors weren't secure and locked. They looked more like a big freezer and a closet. To prevent a surprise, quiet and with careful steps, he stalked toward the unopened doors. He scanned the lab, looking under tables and for any shelf or drawer that could hide a body.

Someone else was in there. He couldn't see them, but he could sense them.

He grabbed the handle of what looked like

a walk-in freezer and dragged it open. A puff of cool air smacked him in the face. Hypnotic white clouds rolled out and around him. See-through freezer compartments lined each side of the space. Vials and boxes filled up each shelf.

And Dr. Hammer sat in the middle of the empty floor tied to a chair and screaming behind the gag in his mouth. The legs slid against the floor as he bounced and struggled to get free.

Liam shoved his foot in the door to prop it open. "Maura, in here."

She came running. With one look at Dr. Hammer and the room, she sized up the problem. "There's probably an emergency release, but I'll need something to hold the door just in case."

She could skip around in circles for all Liam cared. He kept his gun trained on Hammer. After everything that had happened, Liam knew not to trust this guy. With a quick look around the area, and realizing no one else hid in there, Liam stood in front of the other man.

Dr. Hammer never stopped yelling. He strained against the ropes that bound him.

"Not one more word." Liam's hand hovered over the gag, but he didn't remove it until Hammer nodded in understanding.

As soon as the material slipped out of his mouth, the doctor started giving orders. "Cut me loose right now."

"Why should I?"

Hammer looked past Liam. "Maura. Get me out of these."

She came to a stop beside Liam. "Not until you tell me how you got in them."

"What is wrong with you two?" Hammer's furious scowl traveled between them. "Release me."

Maura didn't appear all that impressed with the guy now. "You're supposed to be dead."

"I was kidnapped, you idiot."

Liam shoved the gun in Hammer's face. "Hey!"

Hammer talked right over the threat and offered one of his own. "Remove the rope this instant or you'll be out of a job."

Liam tried to imagine this guy as some top-secret government weapon. Hard to imagine. "Who put you in here?"

"Why are you asking me questions?" The disdain dripping from Hammer's voice suggested he found Liam unworthy to talk to him. "You can see I've been attacked. Do something."

"Tied up," Liam pointed out.

"Excuse me?"

"Someone tied you up." Liam tried to slip his finger underneath the binding and couldn't. "We want to know why."

"This is nonsense. I demand you let me go."

Maura rolled her eyes at her boss. Whatever hero worship she exhibited in the past was gone now. Her frustrated frown and matching tone all but dismissed the man and his current predicament.

"You can shout all you want, but we're not making one move until you tell us what's going on," she said.

With a clenched jaw and ragged tone, fury poured out of Hammer as he spoke. "Rex Smithfield wanted my research. When I refused to work with him, he blew up the lab and took my findings."

Maura's eyes widened. "And tried to kill me. Don't forget that part."

Hammer shrugged off that piece of information. "You're obviously fine."

Liam wanted to smash the other man's face in for the careless way he wrote off Maura's life. "I can see why you wanted to work with him. He's very supportive."

She crossed her arms in front of her stomach and shook her head. "Not for his personality, I assure you."

"Enough talking. Untie me." Hammer shouted the command.

"Why did you submit the false reports?"

Shock registered on Dr. Hammer's face at Maura's question. "What are you talking about?"

"You told NIH our work failed."

Hammer stumbled over his words. "That was part of Smithfield's plan."

"Where is everyone now?" Liam asked.

Hammer spared Liam only the briefest of glances. "How should I know?"

"Wrong answer." Liam dragged Hammer's chair around so the man saw nothing but Liam's face. He leaned down with his palms on the armrests. "Want to try again?"

"I have two guards in the evening." The words raced out of Hammer now. He spoke so fast, the syllables ran together. "When the electricity switched off, they put me in here and left to take a look. I've been in here ever since. Freezing, I'll have you know."

Maura studied the knots behind the doctor's back. "I don't think he could tie his own arms and legs."

Liam tugged on the end of the rope to test its strength.

"What do you think you're doing?" Hammer asked, clearly appalled at being touched by Liam.

"They're tight." Liam talked over Hammer's head to Maura.

"Of course they're tight." Hammer tried to look behind him but settled for yelling when that failed. "Maura, I demand you get me out of here."

"Oh, we're definitely leaving." Liam didn't know what was going on, but he knew they weren't going to hang around and see how all the pieces fit together. They'd figure that out later, at the police station, while Hammer explained Maura's innocence on the kidnapping and explosion charges.

Hammer lifted his chin. The man acted

like he'd won the conversation. "I should think so."

Liam viewed the discussion differently. "Your arms stay tied."

Chapter Thirteen

"It would appear the game is coming to an end." Smithfield watched the scene inside the freezer with only a speck of interest.

To Dan, those minutes meant everything. He couldn't hear the words but he could see the body language. Liam and Maura were working together. Smithfield made the plotting look easy, but Dan still believed the man sold Maura and Liam short. They had resilience and determination. Dan would bet Liam had figured out Smithfield's game by now.

"It is a shame, really. Turning Hammer had been so easy." Smithfield rewound the tape and then played the freezer-rescue scene again before starting the process over. "Use his wife and the lure of money and he sold out his job and country. The last few days hunting your sister provided almost the same thrill as the unveiling of my company's breakthrough will do."

"You're sick."

"Motivated."

"You're stealing a government find and turning it into a profit-making scheme. It's a matter of benefiting from other people's suffering."

"Do not be naive. You are a businessman. From the information I dug up on you, you appear to be a relatively successful one."

"I don't cheat and accuse innocent women of crimes."

"That only shows your lack of vision. Throughout scientific history there have been sacrifices."

"Like integrity?"

"How noble."

"My sister isn't a bargaining chip."

"No, I find her more interesting than a simple lab experiment."

Dan tried to turn off his mind, to drown out the sound of the other man's voice. "Your plan is never going to work."

"It is already a success. I expect criminal charges to come down against your sister any day. She will not serve any time, of course.

I cannot allow a trial to happen, or for the publicity to turn rancid.

"How can you possibly hope to get away with making two scientists and a security expert disappear?"

"No one is looking in my direction."

"They will."

"I would stay and fight about this but I have an appointment. You see, it's time for me to end this game with your friend and sister." Smithfield removed his earpiece and slid it across the desk to his assistant. "Make sure Mr. Lindsey stays right here while I'm gone."

"He will," she said.

MAURA UNTIED HER BOSS'S LEGS, let him stand up and walk around. She guided him out of the freezer and got him a sweater to help warm him up. She mostly fought the urge to tie the clothing around his neck and pull really tight.

Despite all she'd done for him in the past and all she did now to make him comfortable during a difficult situation, the man never stopped whining. He'd been complaining since the second after the gag came off.

"This is an absolute insult. I insist you free my hands right now." Hammer sat on his couch, but followed every move she made with his eyes and his head.

"No." She picked up his notes and scanned his almost unreadable handwriting.

"Did I say you could look at my computer? At my things?" Hammer sounded outraged that she would dare touch his work.

She wondered how she ever admired this man. "Since I did part of the work on this research, I don't care what you think."

"You were nothing more than a secretary."

Liam smacked Dr. Hammer in the head as he walked back into the room. "One more word and I'm putting the gag back in your mouth."

Anger rushed over Dr. Hammer's face. He turned red from his neck to his receding hairline. "Who do you think you are?"

"The one person who can get you out of here alive. Not that I'm inclined to do so at the moment."

Maura nodded. "I'd listen to him."

Hammer chose another option. "You work for me."

"I did until you blew up the lab and left me inside."

"That was Smithfield," Dr. Hammer insisted.

"I think it's time we let someone else take care of Hammer here."

"What does that mean?"

"The police."

Dread settled deep in her stomach and bubbled there. The police wanted her. Walking right into their hands struck her as a huge mistake. The entire reason she'd gone to Liam was to avoid the police.

"Are you sure?"

"Detective Spanner would love to chat with Hammer about the kidnapping and how he really escaped that explosion. All we have to do is get downstairs and the police will do the rest."

"That's what I'm worried about." That meant guards and guns, and this time with Dr. Hammer attached to their sides. She doubted he would be much help in a firefight. It was hard enough on Liam to watch over her while he planned his strategy.

"Hammer will explain everything and clear your name, won't you, Doctor?"

He sat there with a blank look on his face. "I will handle all of this as soon as you free me."

The cryptic response pricked the sensitive spot at the back of her neck. Something about the nonanswer sent anxiety whirring through her.

From his frown, Liam appeared to pick up on the note of dishonesty in Dr. Hammer's voice. "Tell us where the second exit is."

"What are you talking about?" Dr. Hammer asked.

Liam didn't let the biting response stop him. "You entered the lab through your private apartment. How did other people get in?"

"I have been confined to the lab. It's not as if I've been rewarded with visiting hours."

"Someone brought you food. I'd guess Smithfield stopped by to discuss expectations. Hell, how did the two guards get in when they came to attack you?" Liam fiddled with the back of his phone. "Give me something."

The real answer hit Maura like a punch in the gut. She spent hours tied to the lab. For years, she justified her removal from the real world by saying her work had a higher purpose. She argued with Dan, missed events and skipped her college years in favor of rushing through and getting to the career she longed to experience.

The work mattered, and the rush of finding her way through a seemingly impossible scientific question never faded, but her motivation had been wrong. She wanted to please this man, The Dr. Langdon Hammer. She wanted to be him and move in his quiet, special world. She didn't need the praise or her name on research papers. She actually convinced herself that being in his presence and soaking in his brilliance was enough for her.

And now she knew he was a liar and a cheat.

"You're in on it with Smithfield." The truth of the words hit her as she said them.

Dr. Hammer scoffed. "That's ridiculous. Look at me."

She had doubted him as she watched him walk out of the burning lab without an ounce of fear or a second of concern for her. Still, a part of her believed in him and searched for a reasonable explanation. Now she knew better.

Her gaze fell on Liam. Now she knew that true heroes didn't view themselves that way.

They went about their lives. They stepped up. They failed and they got back up.

She turned her wrath back on her boss, just let it flow through her until it took over, fueling her for the hardships they still had to overcome. "You wanted the money and didn't want to share the prestige with the government. But I still don't understand how you planned to pull this off. Smithfield will get all of the credit for your findings. After everything, how can you live with that?"

"Your conclusions, as usual, do not match the wealth of information in front of you." Dr. Hammer shook his head. "It is one of your more pronounced weaknesses."

Liam ground the end of his gun against Dr. Hammer's thigh. "Let's stick to Maura's topic."

"What are you doing?" Dr. Hammer's anger turned to a girlish squeal as Liam pressed the gun tighter against his pants.

"You have ten seconds to tell me or I'll shoot your kneecap off."

"He wouldn't." Dr. Hammer frowned at her. "Talk to your boyfriend."

Maura waited for a surge of sympathy to hit her, but it never came. Dr. Hammer had dragged them all into a disaster and still acted like the aggrieved party. "I'm not going to stop him, so don't look at me."

"Before you make your decision, you may want to know that I was kicked off the police force for worse than this," Liam said.

Dr. Hammer's gaze flew around the room. If he expected someone to barge in and rescue him, it wasn't happening.

Liam dug the barrel in even deeper. "Your decision?"

"Behind the bookshelf in the supply closet."

"I thought you'd see reason." He winked at Maura. "Let's go."

LIAM TOOK TWO STEPS before the refined voice boomed in his earpiece.

"You are going to leave Dr. Hammer in his apartment and walk through the door behind the bookshelf."

The sinister calm of the man's voice stopped Liam's step and shook his insides. Maura was too busy gathering up the notes on Dr. Hammer's desk to notice the problem. Liam lowered his head so he wouldn't give anything away. Not until he knew what was going on.

"I have been listening in," the deep voice said. "It was very handy of you to steal my guard's microphone and then carry it around with you."

Liam closed his eyes in anguish. He'd led the man right to them. Given them every plan and scheme. No wonder it felt as if he knew what they would do before they did it. He only hoped the guy thought the talk about the police was a bluff.

"You would be wise not to tell Dr. Lindsey you can hear me." There was a brief pause. "I would hate to have to kill her after all you have done to keep her alive."

Sweat gathered on Liam's forehead. When he glanced up he saw Dr. Hammer staring at him. All fear had left his face to be replaced with a knowing smirk. One that begged for Liam to kill him.

Being tied up was a ruse to get them in there and set up something for them outside. Liam felt sure of that.

"I will not hesitate to kill her brother, either. Dan, is it? He has been enjoying the show with me. Well, that is the wrong word since it appears he did not know about your crush on his baby sister." A tsk-tsking sound echoed in the mike. "She is a bit young for you, yes?"

Liam's worst fears came true. There was a camera trained on them. This guy could see and hear everything.

"You and your girlfriend have caused me enough trouble. If she had simply perished in the fire as planned, all of this would be moot. She would have taken the blame, gone down as a minor Internet celebrity to the animal protection crowd that hates these sorts of experiments, and that would have been the end."

Liam tried to hide his face as he visually searched the room for a hidden camera. It could be anything from the coffeepot to the amateur painting on the wall.

"Dr. Hammer has work to do. I can no longer afford to have him disrupted this way, and your girlfriend clearly is a distraction. A bit dangerous, as well. Brains on a woman often lead to that problem."

Liam shook his head. A misogynist loser planned to kill all of them, regardless of the mess and explanations something like that would cause. Only Hammer would get out alive, and that was only because the man needed him. Once that changed, Hammer would be gone, too.

Liam knew this guy's type, had dealt with smooth-talking psychopaths his entire professional life. He'd even worked for a few.

The man, Rex Smithfield, if Liam had to guess, looked the part of functional businessman but on the inside, Smithfield craved a different type of domination. He wanted to control people and thrived on his ability to do so. Liam would use that against him. Let Smithfield think he had them cornered. Buy enough time to find Dan and get Maura out of there.

"Make up an excuse to leave, Mr. Anderson. Her only hope is for you to walk away from her right now."

Liam knew a con job when he saw one. Leaving behind witnesses was not in Smithfield's game plan.

Maura turned around with the papers in her hands just as the voice faded from Liam's ears. She was in tune enough with him that one look at his face and the color seeped out of hers.

"What's wrong?"

He shook his head. "I'm just rethinking my strategy."

"Very good, Mr. Anderson," Smithfield said with some amusement. "I can see why you did so well for yourself following your unfortunate downfall with the police department. Most men would have hid in shame. You started a new life performing the very tasks taught to you by the police force that abandoned you. Very inventive."

The tactic wouldn't work. Liam refused to let this weasel's insults get to him.

"Liam?" One second Maura was across the room and the next she stood right in front of him with her hand on his chest.

The feel of her soothed him. He wanted to share the new information with her, but he couldn't risk her life. He put his hands on her forearms and gave her a gentle push back.

She noticed immediately. Her eyebrows slammed together as she scowled. "Tell me what just happened."

"I made up my mind."

"Fill me in."

"I'm going to go through the door alone."

"What?"

"You and Hammer will stay in here. I'll see if it's clear in the hall and down the stairs. We can't afford another run-in with the guards."

"No way. We are in this together." She ticked off her reasons, getting more worked up as she went. "You promised not to leave me behind or fall into that macho garbage."

He knew that conversation never happened. He was prepared to dump her in a safe house at any point. He'd thought about doing it several times and now realized he should have.

"I did?"

"It was implicit when you handed me the gun."

Did she have to mention that?

He slipped her hands between his palms to calm her back down and stop them from waving in his face. "I need to know there's a safe exit to get you both out of here before we start."

"You're worried about the ambush thing."

"Exactly."

"That's fine but I need to know the plan. You are not doing the lone-wolf thing. You had your chance to run away and didn't take it. Now you're stuck with me."

Her spitfire mode temporarily wiped out his anxiety. "I'm happy to hear that."

"You're not acting like it."

His hands slid down to her waist. Leaning

in, he let his mouth hover over hers. "The strategy is the same as it's always been. Be ready and move fast."

She raised up and pressed her mouth against his in a quick kiss that ended as soon as it began. "That's not much of a plan."

Cuddling her close served a dual purpose, savoring her touch for what could be the last time and hiding his fingers as they tapped on the top of the stun gun. "We have to adjust as new information becomes available."

Confusion raced across her face when he wiggled the weapon free. "True."

He stared at her, willing her to understand something else was happening around them and play along. When she frowned back at him, he kissed her. His mouth traveled over hers, caressing and loving, in a true moment of passion in the midst of a fiery disaster.

As he lifted his head, he slipped the stun gun out of her waistband. Every second of the transfer he hoped she wouldn't ask why, wouldn't blow his subterfuge.

Then something warm and knowing sparked in those chocolate-brown eyes. Her stare didn't drop to her belt and the gun. It moved to his earpiece.

He closed his eyes on a slow blink to let her know she was on the right track. "Do we agree on the strategy?"

"I trust you."

A wealth of emotion hid behind those words. Every part of her body signaled her belief in him. Her intense stare did not let up. Her fingers tightened on his shirt. The energy thrumming through her poured into him.

With a brush of his thumb over her lips, he broke the contact. "Have your gun ready just in case."

She glanced over her shoulder at Dr. Hammer. If she didn't know the rules had changed up until then, the doctor's smug smile would have given it away.

"I have one gun and it will be pointed at Dr. Hammer just in case," she said.

Two. She had two guns and the knife. Liam knew that much. Message sent and received.

With reluctance, Liam pulled away from her, but not before pocketing the slim stun gun. Whoever waited on the other side of the door expected a hail of bullets. They likely wore protective gear to guard against any fire-power he might bring. He'd have a few seconds' advantage before they searched him. In that moment, he'd attack with the weapon they didn't expect.

"Very touching, Mr. Anderson." Smithfield's flat and emotionless tone never changed. It only grew colder and deadlier the more the game progressed.

"Now, move toward the hidden door. Be prepared to surrender the weapon and your girlfriend might live."

Right. The one thing Smithfield couldn't afford to do was leave a witness. Liam knew that much.

"I'll be back in a few minutes, after I have a look around," he said as he walked through the bedroom and into the lab.

"Nicely done, Mr. Anderson. Make her feel secure so she will not be tempted to follow you."

Every cell inside Liam wanted to swear at the man and tell him to shut up. But he refused to give Smithfield that satisfaction. The man enjoyed the suffering portion of his sport. Liam felt certain of that fact. He could hear it in the endless abyss of the other man's dark voice.

Leaving Maura alone with Hammer was the hardest thing he'd ever done. He forced his legs to keep going, but his heart remained back in the room, with her.

Right before he hit the door release he touched his thumb against the button on his phone. Despite the phone blackout, the automated text would show up on Detective Spanner's screen within seconds.

Liam sure hoped the man led with his gut and moved fast.

Liam's gaze never stopped. He looked at the door from edge to edge and sized up all conceivable problems. Getting back in being the biggest potential hurdle.

He slid his palm against his pants, lowering the phone as close to the floor as he could get it without bending over and putting it on the floor. He let it drop, tried to catch it with the corner of his shoe.

The small click of plastic against cement got lost when he pounded on the door. Let whoever was watching think he was banging, trying to get out. With his foot he covered the phone. It would provide the perfect doorstop, provide just enough space for him to wedge his fingers inside and pull it back open when he needed to get back inside.

Just as expected, when the lab door opened,

two guards stood in the hall. One aimed a gun at his head. The other just stood there with a stupid grin on his face. The kind of grin that promised a lot of pain.

"Gentlemen." The door rumbled shut behind Liam as soon as he delivered the greeting.

The metal clank vibrated down to his feet. It sounded so final. Made him worry the phone trick didn't work.

The guard with the weapon took a step forward. "Are you the one who killed Paul?"

Liam assumed Paul was the dead guard in the stairwell at the opposite end of the apartment-lab combination. "Yeah."

"We worked together for a long time."

"He cried like a girl when I shot him."

The other guard took a step forward but his friend motioned him back with the gun. "The boss said your death had to look like an accident. A painful one."

The seemingly unarmed guard smiled then. "But we can do whatever we want to your girlfriend. Think about that while you're dying, smart guy."

Liam tried to think of anything else.

Chapter Fourteen

When Liam lifted her stun gun, Maura had
gotten the message. The trap had been sprung
by the person running Dr. Hammer's life.

They had to launch an offensive strike or
risk being the next set of victims. Fear whipped
up inside her at the thought. Her chest felt
like a battle waged in there. Every time she
breathed in, a harsh lump of air got trapped
in her lungs.

Nothing, not even the fear of dying, com-
pared to the nightmare scenarios that ran
through her mind while she watched Liam
walk away. All she wanted to do was run
after him and beg his forgiveness for putting
them in this situation. She should have left
him alone and figured out the problem on her
own. Dragging him back into her life after all
these years was unfair.

But she couldn't regret it, not all of it, not when seeing him and getting to know him as a man sparked something to life inside her.

She had lusted after him with a crush as a teenager, spun wild and grown-up fantasies about him taking her with him as he started his life in another town. The handsome jock with the broad shoulders and infectious smile. He represented everything carefree and open about life.

The exact opposite of her.

She adored her family, but the romanticized version of him that played in her head meant freedom. With him, she could forget about studying and the college decisions that were more complicated than she was prepared to make at fifteen. He was the way for her to hold on to her youth.

When he crushed her hopes, she lost it all. She gave in to the practical side of her and never looked back. For years, she blamed him for the direction of her life. She relished her work but resented it, too. Resented him.

It all seemed so ridiculous now. It was as if the emotional side of her failed to mature and let go while the rest of her grew up. Deep inside, she believed if she piled all of the hurt and responsibility on him, she didn't have to deal with the pieces of normal life she'd forfeited.

She understood now how unfair she'd been. She judged him for choices he'd made in his twenties and she'd made her entire life, dragging all of that baggage with her and letting it poison the part of her outside the lab. Dan paid the price when she kept them all separate, but so did she. She missed out on getting to know the real Liam.

She saw him now with a woman's perspective. She counted on his loyalty and basked in his strength. Rock solid, handsome and good. She loved him this time, not as the foolish girl who confused hormones for love, but as a woman who knew the difference.

That's why seeing him go into the lab with the calm assurance of someone bent on rescuing her one last time nearly killed her. He was prepared to die for her.

"He's not coming back," Dr. Hammer said with a chuckle.

Her boss's newfound confidence was her second clue. He knew who or what controlled Liam. The knowledge filled Dr. Hammer with a false bravado.

"I thought you were pretending to be innocent in all of this." She held her gun at her side. If she pointed it at his head she might shoot him.

"Smithfield made me an offer I couldn't refuse."

Disgust filled her. She had guessed at the cause—money—but hearing it made it real. "You sold out to the highest bidder."

"NIH couldn't possibly handle the requests my research will garner. After all I poured into this work, I can't see it buried and red-taped to death by a bureaucracy that consistently fails to recognize true brilliance."

"You've spent too much time reading your résumé."

He talked right over her as if she didn't even exist. "I needed a private firm with significant resources to highlight the findings."

His ego proved to be his downfall. He was just one in a long line of smart men who got tripped up by his elevated self-worth.

She should have been surprised, but she wasn't. He was a sad little man with nothing to sustain him but work. Turning over the progression of her life scared her a bit. Except for the overblown ego, she walked the same path, started measuring every part of her life by one aspect.

That would stop today. She refused to follow Dr. Hammer's lonely and destructive personal path. There was a way to have it all and she would find it.

"You've lost your mind and your integrity," she said, forcing her mind to stay on the conversation and off Liam and what he might be walking into right this second.

"I simply realized that I should be paid for my work."

"You have half the government and all of the police looking for you. Tom is dead."

Dr. Hammer's mouth went flat. "Who?"

She had to count to ten to keep from flying into a killing rage. "The security guard who worked in your lab for years. Remember him?"

Dr. Hammer had the nerve to nod his head, as if sparing one second of thought or one ounce of sympathy for a man who served him without fail was a hardship. "That was an unfortunate part of the deal."

"Do you hear yourself? Do you understand what you've become?"

"I believe you told me at your initial

interview that you hoped to be like me one day."

"Not anymore." She tried to see into the lab but the door from the bedroom had closed behind Liam, leaving only the makeshift closet. In that moment she prayed that whatever plan Liam came up with, whatever he hoped to do with that stun gun, worked.

"That's probably for the best. Honestly, I'm not sure you have the dedication it takes to make it in this field."

Dr. Hammer's words pricked at her. He wanted a fight, wanted to insult and degrade her.

She wasn't about to play along. "What about Patricia?"

His half smile vanished. "She is fine."

"She is running around out there trying to find your supposed killer. The government worried about its precious data but she…" The pieces fell together in Maura's head. "Wait a second. This is about her, isn't it?"

"Of course not."

"The quickie wedding. The sudden interest in your career. The fake outrage that I hadn't been arrested."

Dr. Hammer looked everywhere but at her. "I have no idea what you're talking about."

"Sure you do. You being here in this claustrophobic pseudo apartment and not caring about the separation from your young wife." It was so obvious that Maura wondered how she had missed it before. "Patricia is in on this. Maybe even the mastermind."

"I think we've talked enough."

The deep male voice had her spinning to face the front of the apartment. Maura's gun came up with the muzzle pointed at Dr. Hammer's head. She had no idea if she could pull the trigger, but she sure could act like she would.

"Lower the weapon." The man spoke as the door between the apartment and the hall swung closed behind him.

He was tall and what some women might find objectively attractive with the dark hair and eyes.

Maura saw a slithering snake.

She knew, but asked anyway in an attempt to stall for time and allow Liam to get back. She also wanted him to hear voices and tread carefully. "Who are you?"

"Rex Smithfield."

"Untie me." Dr. Hammer directed his order at Smithfield.

He ignored it and focused on her. "You are trespassing."

"That doesn't give you the right to hold me here."

"Then you may view it as good news that your time here is almost over."

Ominous. The way this man phrased things, the feral gleam in his eyes. He scared the crap out of her. "Where's Liam?"

"Dead."

The word crashed through her, breaking down every wall and knocking the breath right out of her. She wanted to bend over. Scream. Punch her fist through something until it bled.

She forced her body to stay upright and plastered a bored expression on her face. This man would pounce on weakness, so she refused to show him any. "That's not true."

"I am afraid it is. He proved very interesting right to the end. One would have thought a man of his background would take the easy way out and let you fight this battle on your own. He is, after all, a coward who let a domestic violence victim get killed by her husband."

The need to defend Liam stole over her before she could stop it. "You don't know anything about him."

"I am surprised you took the chance on him. Seems out of character for you. Dr. Hammer kept insisting you were a pathetic loner without a man. I guess you hid your darker side from your boss."

"Liam is alive." She'd know if he were dead. Something inside her would wither. She still felt his spirit as strong as she did when he wrestled with Detective Spanner on her behalf.

"He is very dead." Smithfield seemed to enjoy saying the words. Not that he smiled. It was more that his eyes brightened at the thought of another killing.

"Unless you bring Liam to me, alive and well, within the next two minutes, I'm going to shoot your prize doctor in the head." She shoved the weapon against the back of Dr. Hammer's skull to prove her point.

The man panicked. He shifted in his chair and tried to wiggle his arms out of their bindings. "Get her away from me."

Smithfield remained calm. "You have grown ever more interesting, Dr. Lindsey."

She let his demeanor feed hers. "And your time is ticking."

"WE'LL TAKE THE GUN." The guard grabbed the weapon from Liam's hand as he spoke.

The dark-haired guard never wavered from his position. Neither let Liam out of his sight, nor lowered the gun. "He has others."

Liam cataloged the arsenal he had on him. Plastic explosives, a second gun, knives, a razor blade and the stun gun. Chances of these two wrestling them all away before he could use one of them was slim. All Liam needed was an opening.

He kept his eyes on the one holding the gun as the other one did a pat down. He started at Liam's feet, quickly found gun number two, all the time describing the horrible things he planned to do with Maura once he got her alone.

Liam blocked it all out, had to. If he let the words fester and take hold, he'd lose control. That meant risking Maura, and he couldn't let that happen.

And he was smart enough to know these

two bruisers depended on him to go wild. They wanted him to make a mistake, give them a reason to unload those weapons right into him.

The guard slipped Liam's knife out of the sheath and threw it on the ground before glancing up at his partner. "Looks like the trespasser came armed for a fight."

It was the pause Liam needed.

He rammed the stun gun into the neck of the guy kneeling on the floor. The prongs made contact for less than a second before Liam pivoted. He shifted his weight and brought his elbow up under the armed guard's hand. A shot rang out, going wide and lodging in the wall behind Liam's head.

While the man on the floor crawled around dazed, the one on his feet didn't stop fighting. Liam tried twice to land the stun gun prongs on the side of the other man's neck, but the guy blocked both attempts.

They grunted and twisted. Both men's hands went to the gun. Liam spun around, putting his back against the man's front in an attempt to get the leverage he needed to pry the weapon from the other man's fingers. He threw his elbows and kicked his shins. The man grunted but did not go down.

Then the guy got in a shot of his own. His knee landed in the center of Liam's back. He heard something crack just before he flew across the hallway and into the far wall. His head spinning, he managed to duck just in time to clear another bullet. It kicked up drywall when it landed. From the look of the spot it would have torn right through his chest.

While in a crouch, Liam slipped his second knife from the band inside his sleeve. He spun around and jabbed the blade deep into the other man's upper thigh. The resulting shout almost blew out Liam's eardrum. The big man wailed as he grabbed his leg.

With his attention scattered, Liam stabbed him a second time, this one in the stomach, just under the edge of his bulletproof vest. To be sure, Liam jabbed the prongs of the stun gun into his shoulder. The zapping didn't stop until the man fell in a heap on the floor.

This one wasn't awake and in pain. He was out. Liam intended to keep it that way.

He lifted the gun out of the man's open palm as the other guard's hand found Liam's weapon on the floor. Liam saw the move out of the corner of his eye and was ready. The off-balance shot hit the guard in the neck. The guy dropped his gun as his hands flew to the spurting wound.

He fell back against the wall. The man's skin was slick from the wetness and his eyes wide and glassy as he fought to breathe. Sitting there, his legs and arms moved and he fought for his life, silently begging for help.

The choking sound, the gurgling of blood. Liam had seen a shot like that before, had lost his job over it. For a second it paralyzed him. The memories flooded his brain, taking him back to that horrible day when a man snapped right in front of him.

When the guard kicked out at Liam, the mental coma snapped. Liam stripped off his shirt, leaving behind only a tee, and pressed it to the wound. When the blood immediately soaked the material, Liam knew the truth. There was nothing he could do. The guy would bleed out in seconds.

Fighting with his conscience, Liam stood up. He tried to ignore the gagging sounds coming from the dying man. He fought to remember all of the threats this guy made to Maura and believed he deserved this vicious end. It was the guard or Maura, and Liam picked her over everyone.

He felt for a pulse in the guard with the leg wound. Nothing. By the time he turned around to see if he could do anything to ease the bleeding man's pain, both men were dead. He stared at the mixing pools of blood and thought about Maura. She would not end up like them. He would die first.

He stepped over the bodies and felt for a crack in the door, an opening of some sort. His fingers fell on a small space, just enough to slip his fingertips through. He wanted to grunt and yell and make whatever noise helped tighten his grip and give him better leverage, but he closed his mouth to keep from making a sound. He did not need another guard showing up to save the day.

The thing weighed a ton. He grabbed and pulled. It moved by fractions of inches. It was as if the metal came alive and fought back. With each strained yank, his muscles grew weaker. He wrenched his shoulder, thought he heard something tear in his wrist right before pain shot down into his fingers.

His body begged for mercy, but he couldn't concede. He inhaled one last time and pictured her smiling face. He would throw every ounce of energy into this tug and pull out with all his might. If he fell over doing it, fine.

At first the door didn't move, and then it started to swing. Momentum worked on his side. Whatever spring mechanism worked this thing went from fighting him to helping him open the door. He was able to get enough space to slip through.

As he stepped, he heard a crunching beneath his foot. He looked down at his broken cell. That wiped out some of his gadgets. It also took away his only access to the outside world. He hoped like hell Spanner got the earlier message and had started rallying the troops to storm the building.

That left one piece of electronics. To keep from giving Smithfield additional help, Liam smashed the earpiece under his foot. If Smithfield wanted to talk to him, he could do it to his face.

Chapter Fifteen

Detective Spanner pulled up to the circular driveway in front of the towering Smithfield Enterprises building. It was a modern monstrosity with floors of glass and an intricate angle at the top to set it apart from the three that surrounded it.

Spotlights usually lit the marble sculpture and garden and water fountains in the circle out front. Tonight, neither worked. For the first time he could remember, the water didn't dance. The place was completely dark. All those floors and not a single light shone in the windows.

He glanced at the businesses nearby and saw that all had at least some lights on. Many had entire floors lit. Not this one.

Seeing the black outline of the building and no life within it had him grabbing for his gun.

There was no law against quiet or darkness, but it felt wrong to him.

He pulled out his phone and read the texts again. First a message from Liam: Hammer at Smithfield Enterprises and Maura in danger.

Then a blueprint of the office building.

Liam sent them for a reason. Picked Spanner over anyone else in order to send a message. Maybe Liam knew Spanner wanted a bit of revenge for getting the jump in the kitchen. Liam had to know Spanner would track him for that one. That meant this was a setup and Spanner was giving Liam one more chance to screw with him.

Or this was a request for help between law enforcement officials.

The feds had taken over the case. They thought Liam and Maura had teamed up to steal Dr. Hammer's findings and make billions in some sort of underground transplant ring. The forensics found in the lab pointed to Maura. Her fingerprints were on the explosive device. What little could be recovered on the office computers showed Maura changing data. A quick look at Liam's house made it clear he had been harboring her. Not that

Spanner needed proof of that one. He saw it with his eyes.

But the pieces fit too neatly for Spanner's comfort. Maura was so clean she squeaked. There was no explanation why she'd turn so far and so fast into another life after all those years of studying. And with her brain, surely she'd know how to hide incriminating evidence.

If she didn't, Liam did. He had worked undercover in narcotics for years and only been back in regular rotation for three weeks before he got stuck in the middle of a domestic shootout. Despite the career-ending accident, the man was a good cop. Nothing in his file suggested he was dirty. Most of the guys on the force thought he took the fall for a supervisor who wouldn't let Liam do his job during a domestic violence call.

And a third person stepped into the fray. Dan had gone missing. He had two policemen on his house at all times, yet he slipped out. For a businessman, he had serious covert skills. They all did.

Either the three of them had pulled an incredible con and fooled everyone around them, or they were being set up to take the fall for a mess they didn't create. If the latter were true, Spanner didn't expect any of them to survive the night. Instinct told him Liam had tried to save his girl and landed butt deep in trouble.

An earlier phone call to the Smithfield offices took Spanner to the after-hours voicemail system. Everything sounded in order. Still, his mouth went dry at the thought of leaving the premises. He could do a short look around and then head out—to satisfy his curiosity.

He jogged up the first set of steps, past the dead fountain, and walked up to the double front doors. First thing he saw was a dead alarm panel. Then he noticed the empty guard station in the lobby.

He called dispatch.

THE SHOTS REVERBERATED throughout the entire floor. When Maura heard them bounce and echo, her body went numb. Every nerve cell stopped firing. Even her heartbeats slowed to a crawl. She hadn't been hit, but she may as well have been. She waited for her blood and vital fluids to puddle on the floor beneath her.

She could see Smithfield's lips move but

everything sounded muffled, as if she had lost her hearing. Shaking her head, she cleared out some of the clouds covering her senses.

"Dr. Lindsey?"

She wanted to crawl into a ball and cry. Better yet, to race up to Smithfield and punch him until he fell or her fists bled.

She wanted to shoot Hammer in the middle of his big head for taking them all down this path.

"Do you believe me now?" Smithfield asked with what she assumed was his version of a smile.

It creeped her out. Everything about this man made her skin itch.

"I can have my men bring your boyfriend's lifeless body in, if you would prefer."

The thought of seeing Liam bloody and broken made her gag on a rush of vomit. She bent over to fight it off then shot straight again to keep her gun on Hammer. It wavered in her hand, but was close enough to do a lot of damage if she fired.

Smithfield laughed. "I guess not."

Still, through all the pain and everything she heard and saw she didn't feel the end. It was as if Liam's life force pumped inside her, reassuring her he was fine. Hope blossomed in her heart. Her head had gone into shutdown mode, but something inside her soared with a surety his blood still pumped.

She either waded in a full pool of denial or Liam pulled off a miracle. She prayed for the latter.

"You are not any better off now than you were two seconds ago," she said in a voice she didn't recognize. The firm tone suggested far more control than she felt from her quivering insides.

"Your boyfriend is dead and you show very little reaction." Smithfield pursed his lips together. "Interesting."

"The countdown to Dr. Hammer's death is still on." She now knew she could do it. If it meant staying alive and getting Liam the medical attention he needed, she would do it. If she could only have one choice, she'd pick him. She wanted him safe. Putting a bullet right into Dr. Hammer's impressive brain wasn't too big a price to pay to make that happen.

"Do something, damn you," the doctor hissed out at Smithfield.

Smithfield's gaze stayed locked on her. "It

would seem to me you underestimated your assistant, Hammer."

People had been doing that her entire life. She hated it, but it never surprised her. Dr. Hammer had never hidden his distaste for her. She was female and young and inferior. At the time, she viewed the job as an opportunity to prove him wrong. Now she saw that his ignorance might have, in some strange way, saved her.

She vowed not to blow that extra chance at life now. "You need to make a choice, Smithfield."

"Call me Rex."

"Never."

Smithfield shrugged. "Well, then, I feel I must point out if Hammer dies, you die."

"Fine with me."

In a first real show of emotion, Smithfield's eyebrows lifted at her terse response. "I doubt you are so cavalier about your life."

"I have nothing left to lose. You took the one man who meant everything to me." When Smithfield tried to butt in with his pontificating crap, she talked over him. "You, however, have everything to lose. Your pet project and all the money that comes with him will be gone. The research won't do much good without Dr. Hammer to interpret it."

"Smithfield." Hammer called out the warning but stopped after one word.

Smithfield gave her an abbreviated bow. "Very well reasoned."

"Then put down your gun."

"I would, except for one small thing."

He was too confident, too convinced he would win this battle. Maura braced for the bad news she knew he held back until the time came to pounce.

"What?"

"My trump card. His name is Dan, I believe."

Her blood dripped icy cold. She had just tricked her brain into thinking Liam crawled out of the ambush and was fine. Now she had to worry about Dan. Poor innocent Dan who sat in his house grieving while all of this spun out around him.

"What have you done?" she asked as panic filled her voice.

"Nothing yet."

It had to be a trick. There was no way Smithfield was in the business of plucking innocent citizens right off the street. Not when the police had staked out Dan's house looking for her. He had to be safe.

"I am willing to offer proof." Smithfield took a cell phone out of his pocket and pressed a few buttons before sliding it across the floor to her.

She caught it under her foot.

Smithfield watched her every move. "Do not get excited. You cannot call out. This is for example purposes only."

Without taking her eyes off him, she bent down and grabbed the phone. A brief glance told her what she needed to know. Dan sat in what looked like a bare, empty office tied to a chair and struggling to get free.

The phone dropped from her hand.

"Do you believe me now?" Smithfield took a step closer, shortening the gap between them to about five feet. "If you do manage to get a shot off and into Dr. Hammer, which I do not think you have the nerve to do, I will kill you and then go after Dan. You cannot win this fight."

She glanced at Dr. Hammer. Even though his benefactor had the upper hand, terror all but streamed out of his pores. His beady eyes scanned the room as if looking for an easy escape. Maybe Dr. Hammer crawled into bed with Smithfield, but he was smart enough to know the man could turn on him at any second.

"How are you going to hide all of the bodies?" she asked.

"Simple. You and your renegade cop kidnapped Dr. Hammer in an attempt to financially benefit from his findings. You had been changing the research results to hide the doctor's success so that you could claim it as your own. When Hammer finally emerged from his seclusion, he realized what you were doing and you kidnapped him." Smithfield ran through the plot with such clarity.

Maura wondered if the man now believed his outrageous tale. "The evidence all points to me."

Smithfield nodded. "Of course. Your brother tried to stop you, a shoot-out occurred. All of the forensics will support the story, but I am sure you understood that part already."

She went for the last card she had. If she could break them apart, get Dr. Hammer panicked and working for her, if only so he thought he had a chance to live, she might be able to stall long enough to figure out a way out of the room without getting shot.

"You're going to kill him after you're done with us." She stared at Dr. Hammer while she said it.

"In name only. Langdon Hammer will die a scientific hero. One of my employees will take over the research on a private level."

She shook her head. "Once you have what you need, you will kill him."

Dr. Hammer started shifting and fidgeting again. "Untie me."

"He can't take the risk of letting you live and spoil his scheme." She shifted until she stood directly behind Hammer, whispering the heavy dose of reality into his ear.

The position gave her a good view of both doors. She almost did a double take when she realized the door from the bedroom to the lab was open halfway. A few minutes ago, she glanced over and tried to see what was happening with Liam. At that point, it was closed.

Relief soared through her. Liam was alive. She felt the truth with every part of her body. One of the guards would have walked in and taken the gun from her. No, this was Liam.

He'd somehow dodged the bullets and come back for her.

"You will lower the gun or I will tell my assistant to kill your brother." Smithfield nodded toward the phone on the floor in front of Dr, Hammer's feet. "You can even watch as it happens."

Smithfield slipped another phone out of his pocket. "Well, Dr. Lindsey? Have you made a decision about what means more to you?"

"Get down!" Liam's shout filled the room just before the gunfire.

It all happened so fast. Smithfield started shooting in the direction of Liam's voice. Bullets passed over her head and in every direction. She ducked behind Hammer's chair when shots smashed into the coffee table behind her.

The booming blasts deafened her. She wanted to throw her hands over her ears, but she kept them on the gun instead. The smell of sulfur filled the air. The room shook as if it were breaking apart from the inside out. If Smithfield came around Hammer, she would shoot them both.

She strained to listen and figure out where everyone stood. Drywall dust kicked up in every direction. Glass shattered then rained down in pieces on the hard floor. Furniture fell. She blinked to keep her vision clear.

She heard the shuffling of feet, felt Dr. Hammer's body flinch a few times as he yelled for the shooting to stop. Then nothing.

The fight stopped as fast as it had started. When the quiet descended, Liam grabbed her arm.

She almost shot him.

The touch of his fingers warmed her from the outside in. She flew into his arms before he could brace for the blow. "Liam!"

Dragging her hands over his head and face, she convinced herself he'd stayed in one piece through the battle. She kissed him, forgetting all about the lurking danger and gun at her side.

"It's okay. It's me." He said the words over and over against her lips before pushing back and looking her up and down. "Were you hit?"

She glanced down. Didn't see or feel anything. "Except for getting showered with some glass shards, I'm fine."

"Good."

He switched from happy-to-see-her to all

business. The police officer in him, calm and in control, took the lead as he scanned the room's damage.

"How did you get away from the guards?" She had lived every second in fear after she heard those gunshots. Not being able to see him killed her.

"Your stun gun helped." Liam stepped around her and went to Hammer's chair.

A haze hung over the room but it didn't block her view of the damage. Bullet holes littered the walls. Furniture was shredded and turned over. It amazed her that two men had done all of this in a matter of a minute.

"You mean they're dead." She didn't ask it as a question because she didn't have to. The grim line of Liam's mouth clued her in.

Searching down deep, she wanted to feel sorry for the guards, for their families, but she couldn't muster a tear. Not after the last few days. Not after sitting hunched over wondering if the man she loved would survive the latest attack.

"So is your boss." Liam stared at Dr. Hammer.

For the first time she noticed his wounds. Holes in his chest and blood on his shirt. It trickled out of the corner of his mouth. And those dead dark eyes.

Sorrow and relief warred inside her. "Is he?"

Liam let his fingertips drop from Hammer's throat. "He's gone."

She bit back the confusing mix of feelings that assailed her. So much wasted talent and all of this over greed. But she could mourn for the Dr. Hammer she thought she knew later.

Right now she had a bigger problem. "Where's Smithfield?"

"Running." Liam hunkered down near the spot on the floor where Smithfield stood before the shooting started. Liam stared at a mark then picked up the cell Smithfield dropped.

"What are you doing?"

"Gathering intel."

"What does that…" The auxiliary power blinked off. "Now what?"

"Smithfield. He's covering his tracks." Liam turned on his flashlight as he stood up.

"What else does he have to hide?"

"Blood."

"Meaning?"

"I hit him. It's all over the floor."

"Do you think he's dead?" It scared her how free and happy the idea made her.

She didn't want to be that person or take pleasure in the slicing pain of others, but her heart yearned for revenge. Just thinking about all that could happen, all that still might, made any sympathy for the man evaporate. He and Dr. Hammer created the mess. She was stuck living it.

"I think he's on his way to Dan and doesn't want us to track him," Liam explained.

The terror nearly overwhelmed her. She didn't realize her knees had given out until she felt Liam's strong arm wrap around her waist. "In all the yelling and gunfire I forgot about Dan. What's wrong with me?"

"We're going to get to Dan in time."

"How can you know that?"

Liam brushed the backs of his fingers across her cheek. "I feel lucky today."

Chapter Sixteen

Detective Spanner stood in the middle of a stairwell when the safety lights turned off. He had tried the elevator, the phones and every door on the lobby floor. This place was locked down tighter than most prisons.

That part didn't disturb him. It was the lack of noise. Even after hours he expected something. The buzz of the HVAC system, a radio from the security detail—something. Even turned down he could hear the chatter on the police radio hooked to his belt, yet from all these floors, not one sound.

The place felt abandoned, as if all humans had been wiped out and removed.

Shouldn't someone in a multi-billion-dollar company work late? Calls to the building—even using the back-line numbers—turned up nothing.

He was all for solid soundproofing, but this level of quiet went beyond that. This was a deadly silence. But something lived and breathed within these walls. He could feel it.

He wanted to write this off as a wild-goose chase, but he knew better. Liam had called him here for a reason. He needed help. He wouldn't risk getting Maura caught if he didn't.

Spanner unsnapped the radio and clicked on the button. "I need backup at Smithfield Enterprises. Now."

LIAM KEPT THE BEAM OF LIGHT on the blood trail and his eyes straight ahead. Smithfield could jump out of any corner or doorway. He could swing around behind them and grab Maura. The only lead they had were the drops leading to the emergency staircase at the opposite end of the hall from where the dead guards lay.

Slow and steady they shuffled toward the door. Maura's death grip on the back of his shirt made maneuvering rough. Normally, he would have complained and made sure he had as full a range of motion as possible. Since he'd almost lost her, stood right there and saw

Smithfield aim at her, he planned to hold her close for a while.

"We're almost there," she whispered against the back of his neck.

She probably thought the running commentary of their location helped. It drove him nuts. Every time she spoke, it broke his concentration. And the warm breath blowing against his neck had him thinking about anything except killing bad guys.

But he understood. Sharing their body heat reminded her they were still alive. They both needed that comfort.

The relief that broke across her face when she saw him, the way she threw her body into his arms refilled the empty well inside him. Those same thankful feelings at seeing her uninjured swirled in him, too.

If they got out of this, he was going to change. No more dangerous assignments. No more letting her push him away. He planned to be a part of her life, to earn the right to be with her.

Those were the promises he made while he stood flat against that bedroom wall and bargained with the universe for her life. He still meant them, but they would both need to adjust. He wanted this Maura. The one that gave herself over to a cause and didn't hide in a lab. The real woman, fresh and smart and beautiful and strong. He had to hope she saw it now, that she understood who she was and what she had to offer.

"Finally," she said under her breath as they reached the door.

The blood dribbled here in a puddle as if Smithfield had waited for them to come out into the hallway and take a shot. For whatever reason, he abandoned his post.

Liam believed that meant he hadn't gotten far. He pulled her away from him. "Step back."

Instead, she slid her back against the wall and faced him. "I'm ready."

She said it with such conviction that he believed it. Or he would have if the gun didn't shake in her fingers.

"I go first." He mouthed the words and waited for her to nod in agreement.

The sound of the door opening, metal clanking against metal, ricocheted down the stairwell. No way were they going to sneak up on Smithfield with that noise. He had boobytrapped the door somehow to warn of their coming. Who knew what other goodies they might find.

Liam stepped over the threshold and Maura swung in behind him.

"Up or down?" she asked in a voice that barely registered above a breath.

Liam saw the drops continue down the stairs. "Wait a second." When he glanced up the stairs, he saw a line of blood there, too.

"What is it?" she asked.

"He walked both ways to throw us off."

Maura inhaled as if weighing the options in her head. "He couldn't have made a fake trail for very long before turning around."

"I agree. You stay here." He turned to jog up the steps. No need to be quiet now that Smithfield knew he was being followed.

She grabbed Liam's arm before he could start his run. "We don't have time for that. I'll go up one flight and see. You go down."

"Out of the question." He'd separated from her once and they'd both nearly paid the price. "We stick together."

"We're talking about Dan's life here. He could already be…"

"He's not."

"How do you know?"

"Smithfield doesn't have a way to communicate with his assistant. He gave you one phone and dropped the other. What are the chances there were three?"

"None." She scooted around him and started up the stairs.

"Maura!"

She ignored his harsh whisper. "Just go."

He hesitated, hating to be away from her again. Good thing he was fast and in good shape. Despite all the activity, adrenaline still pumped through him until the beats of his heart blended together.

"Liam, come here."

He took the steps two at a time to get to her. On the landing of the sixth floor, the blood trail slipped under the door. Unless Smithfield spent a lot of time faking a trail, he was on this floor somewhere.

Opening the door only by inches, Liam glanced down the long hall. Being at the end of the corridor, he had one direction to cover. Only darkness greeted him. To call out Smithfield, Liam did a quick shine of the light into the hallway. If the man saw it, he might shoot or at least shift and give away his location.

Nothing.

Liam pushed on the door and entered the empty corridor, holding it open long enough for Maura to slip in behind him. The blood trail went up and down the floor. This line threw drops on the walls and doors. From the shape, Smithfield had been running when he faked this clue.

"Where is he?" she asked.

"Dunno."

Liam didn't see any lights under any of the doors, but knew that didn't mean anything. There were no cracks below, which meant he had to engage in old-fashioned detective work to reason out which door to open. He doubted he would get more than one chance.

She lifted up on her toes and brought her mouth close to his ear. "The floor schematics."

He turned his head and frowned over at her, letting her know he had no clue what she was getting at.

She nibbled on her bottom lip before spilling her suggestion. "Look for an unoccupied room."

The strategy made sense. Problem was he'd sacrificed the cell as a doorstop to get back into the lab. He tried to call up the building's tech blueprints from memory but it didn't work.

She picked her phone out of her pocket and handed it to him. The small readout was smudged but the crystal was otherwise fine. She breathed over his shoulder as he pushed the buttons searching for a dial tone. Something blocked the phone signal out, making calls for help impossible, but he could call up the memo function and look at the tech department's layout of the floor.

Exactly one room on the sixth floor remained empty. Six-fifteen.

They stalked down the hallway and stopped in front of the door. The blood pool was thicker here. Wherever Smithfield got hit, he was losing blood and fast. He'd need to call in a doctor or ambulance soon. That meant little time to launch his elaborate plan.

This was one opportunity Liam would not squander. He motioned for her to duck down and mirrored her stance on the opposite side of the doorway.

Caught and trapped, Smithfield should come out firing. That was Liam's hope. Give the man a target, then swoop in.

Liam pointed to the doorknob. He'd bet this

one would be unlocked. Smithfield wanted an audience for this showdown. He wanted to flash his masterpiece then play the hero in his twisted fantasy by killing them all. For him, that was the only way for the game to end. Liam preferred a different plot.

He held up his finger for a three count. When he reached one, Maura closed her eyes and pulled. The door shot open, actually knocked Maura over backward on her butt.

Light spilled out of the room as shots rang out above Liam's head. They went wild and came in rapid succession. It was the gunfire of a man in full panic. A guy in the middle of a death spiral.

Liam waited exactly one second after the noise started before crawling into the room. His first shot hit Smithfield in the foot. While the man yelled and jumped, Liam stood up and fired the second shot right into the middle of Smithfield's forehead.

He went from openmouthed shocked to dead. No fanfare or special effects. He just dropped to the floor behind Dan's chair.

Dan. The battery-operated light in this room made it easy to see. Alive and swearing, his friend pulled against his bound wrists as if trying to communicate something.

Liam felt all the stress inside him let go. He hadn't cried in decades, not since he lost his mom, but was on the verge for the second time in an hour today. The relief hit him that hard.

"I've got you." He put the gun on the desk and barely got the gag off Dan when he started screaming.

"Maura!"

Liam whipped around in time to see a woman slip her slim arm around Maura's neck in a choke hold. The edge of a knife pointed at her soft skin. Stunned, and his body exhausted from all of the activities of the last few hours, the sight didn't register in his brain. He saw the furious blonde and the wide-eyed fury in Maura's eyes. None of it made sense.

"Who the hell are you?" He reached for the gun until the unknown woman shook her head.

Dan answered. "She's Smithfield's assistant."

Liam took in the expensive clothes and fancy upsweep of hair. This was no hourly administrative assistant. This was a woman who likely had never worked a day in her life, except for hours between the sheets. She reeked of money and wasted time.

"I don't think so," Liam said.

"Patricia Hammer." As soon as the words left Maura's mouth, the woman tightened her arm and choked them off.

Seeing Maura in peril again brought Liam back to the present. The remaining fog cleared and his body switched to high alert.

If one more person pawed Maura today or ever, he was going to go off in a frenzy of fists and violence. He had seen enough for a lifetime. His muscles ached and a headache hammered away at his skull, but he could fight off anyone who hurt her.

Despite the fresh anger flooding through him, he reined it in. He needed to hold on for a few more minutes, or at least until he figured out how to pry the knife from the woman's fingers.

"You're the angry wife," he said. "I guess we know why you were so upset about the bombing. It was all part of the plan."

Patricia Hammer had the look of an animal, trapped and hunted. Possessed. The tension showed on every line of her face, pulling around her mouth and eyes. Liam had no idea how old the woman was, except that Maura described her as young. Whatever the number, the years were catching up by the minute.

"Stop moving or I will kill her." Patricia spat out the threat.

"Okay." He angled his body so that he could cut the ropes around Dan's wrists.

The movement got Patricia's attention. "What are you doing there?"

"Just letting him breathe a bit."

"Stand still." The knife hovered too close to Maura's neck for comfort.

"You got it." Liam made the cut and shifted back into his old position. "What's your play here, Patricia?"

"Let me worry about that."

"Smithfield is dead. Your husband is dead. There are dead guards all over this building." The body count sounded overwhelming as he added it up.

"Only Langdon's death matters. It ruins everything."

How romantic. "Where are you going and how do you plan to get there?"

"I'm taking her." Patricia altered her hold.

"I don't think so." Maura said with a snort

then winced when Patricia tightened her vise grip.

Liam tried to talk even slower. The alarms in his head kept ringing. Adrenaline pooled inside him just waiting for the chance to fuel his next move.

With his gun on the table and Maura in danger, Liam decided to take a little more time weighing his options. "We can work this out."

A crazed look crossed Patricia's face. It was the desperate look of a woman with little left to lose. "It's settled."

"Patricia, you're a smart woman. You know this won't work."

"Maura knows Langdon's formulas. She can recreate the experiments and keep the work alive."

Just when he thought the situation couldn't get stranger, Patricia lowered the bar. "You think Maura is going to work for you."

"No way." Maura's words were cut off when the knife pricked her.

"Shut up!" Patricia's shrieking scream echoed through the small office.

Liam froze at the sight of Maura's deep red blood. The only part of him that moved was his hand, which pressed down in what he hoped was a calming gesture. "Easy now."

Patricia's wild gaze darted around the room. "I am going to take her and leave. I have all of Langdon's notes at home."

He tried for reasonable even though he knew that train had left Patricia's station long ago. "You'll need a space. I saw all of that fancy lab equipment upstairs. It's not going to be easy recreating that."

"There will be plenty of people willing to bankroll the research. Finding Smithfield was the easy part."

"You were behind all of this."

"You think Langdon set this up?" Patricia threw her head back and laughed. "The man was inept out of the lab."

Liam nodded. "I've heard."

"Yes, she knows. Don't you?" Patricia stared at Maura. "He couldn't do anything without us, could he?"

Maura glanced at Liam as if asking permission to talk. Clearly the cut scared her. Made sense since it terrified him, and from the sound of Dan's tapping foot, he was a nervous wreck, as well.

Liam gave her a slight nod and telegraphed

a look he hoped Maura interpreted as telling her to tread carefully.

"He needed you, Patricia. You made him a better scientist." Maura's soothing voice did nothing to calm the crazed woman behind her.

"Of course I did."

"But I'm not him. I don't have his expertise. He told me all the time I was nothing more than an assistant, a glorified secretary. He believed I was beneath him and certainly not a threat to his work."

Liam's heart ached for Maura. The words ripped out of her in a way that he knew they were true. Having sacrificed so much, she still had to fight so hard.

"He picked you," Patricia insisted.

Maura grabbed on to the other woman's arms when she started to drag them both backward. "But he didn't ask me to come here with him."

"That was Smithfield's decision. He thought too many people in on the secret meant the secret would be harder to keep."

Liam fought to keep his mouth closed. This idiotic woman actually thought she could pull

Maura out of there and set her up in a lab. Turn her into a virtual slave.

Patricia's panicked steps worried him but if she shifted a bit more, he should be able to get to his gun without it being so obvious. He just had to keep her talking. "He wanted to frame Maura for your husband's death."

"It was a practical solution." Patricia's slide continued as she closed in on the door frame. "But she's shown her resiliency. I think your girlfriend and I will make a good team."

Maura's gaze shot to her brother.

Liam didn't turn around to see his reaction to the news. They'd slap a name on their relationship after this lunatic was in prison.

Patricia leaned against the door frame. "We're leaving."

Liam shook his head. "I can't let that happen. She means too much to me to let her walk away, even if it is for work."

"I won't go back to the way things were before. Scraping by and waiting. Langdon made me promises. We had a deal."

The glimpse into the Hammer marriage made Liam shake his head. A lonely man locked in a studio. An aging woman worried she couldn't depend on her looks much longer.

The whole thing was pathetic and maddening. Whenever two limited people met and fractured, disaster followed. He'd seen it a million times. But the scene unfolding in front of him now was new.

"For every step you take, I'll take one." He stepped closer to Patricia, stopping when his back was to the desk, with his gun right behind him.

The knife wobbled. "One more move and I'll kill her."

Chapter Seventeen

Detective Spanner started panting by the time he hit the sixth-floor landing. He had ventured onto every floor, cracked the door and listened for any noise in the hall. Five times and nothing. This was the sixth. From the fourth until here his flashlight picked up a trail of blood on the floor. The line seemed to stop here. He hoped he'd get lucky this time.

After this, he planned to hit the gym more regularly. Climbing the stairs without making a sound and while keeping his breathing shallow made his heart thump.

He flicked off his light and listened. He thought he picked up muffled voices, but his imagination had taken flight in the dark building. He should have waited downstairs for backup. Would have, but the patter in his gut told him to get moving.

The door barely slipped open when the voices reached him. He recognized Maura and Liam. The third was the most interesting. After all of those threats to have his job and go over his head, he heard that husky tone in his sleep. Patricia Hammer wasn't whining and bossing people around now. She was threatening them.

Turned out Ms. Highbrow could add something besides trophy wife to her résumé. If Spanner had anything to say about it, and he would at trial, she'd also be a convict.

The thought made him smile.

He couldn't see around the door or tell if Patricia was in the hallway. He didn't want to rush in and get anyone hurt. He also didn't want to wait one beat too long and have to explain to someone's next of kin the reason for the body bag.

He slipped the toe of his shoe into the door's edge and listened. Liam had brought him here for a reason. Spanner didn't intend to let him down.

MAURA THOUGHT HER NECK would break. This scrawny little woman must have spent some quality time in the weight room because she had the strength of one of Smithfield's massive male guards. It didn't help that she balanced Maura's neck in the crook of her elbow. Every time Patricia shifted, Maura got a bone shoved into her throat. Several times she bit back a gag.

She tried to stay strong for the two men staring at her in horror. Dan's normally tan skin had blanched chalky-white. He had a death grip on the edge of the desk and looked ready to jump up and throw his body in front of hers at any minute.

And Liam. Strong, loving Liam. He shifted his weight around and kept moving. He resembled a caged beast.

Maura loved them both so much. She feared Patricia's knife mostly because of what her death or injury would do to the men in her life.

But she by no means was ready to die. Absolutely not. She would take this blond creature out with her if she had to. Even now, Maura plotted how to get the woman close enough to the wall to smash her head against it. That sort of thing worked in movies. Maura had no idea if it was a reasonable alternative in real life.

She listened to Liam's calm voice. The gentle

sound could lull even the wildest animal into a deep sleep. It seemed to have little effect on Patricia. The woman was lost in this strange money fantasyland.

Maura knew better than to be fooled by Liam's demeanor. He might look almost disinterested in the horror playing out in front of him, but that wasn't true. Liam wasn't about to let this woman leave the floor.

Maura loved him for so many things. Strength she never knew she had flowed through her when she was around him. But mostly she loved his determination. For a man who professed to hang up his hero status, the role continued to fit to perfection.

Patricia slipped them around the door and into the hall before Maura could get enough of a grip to throw her off balance. Walking backward proved awkward. Maura helped the process by dragging her feet and trying to tangle her sneakers in the other woman's high heels.

"Patricia, where are you going?" Liam asked the question as his head peeked around the corner. His hand stayed behind his back.

Dan followed, holding the only light in the entire building. He raised it, flooding the corridor and allowing her to see everyone's hands and faces.

Maura had been with Liam enough over the last few days to know he held a weapon. He wouldn't walk into the corridor unarmed.

"Do not follow us." Patricia shook the knife right next to Maura's nose.

She pulled back, trying to increase the distance between the blade and her skin. She'd already felt the sting of the knife and was determined not to do that a second time.

Liam held up both hands in mock surrender. "I told you I can't let you take Maura."

Maura lost track of the gun. Maybe that was the point. Keep Patricia guessing. Did Dan have it or did Liam? She had no idea but she drew comfort from watching them stand together not ten feet away. For every step back Patricia took, they took one forward.

Patricia shook her head. "You don't have a choice."

"That's where you're wrong. There's always another option." Liam directed his gaze right at Maura. "Right?"

She had no idea what Liam was trying to tell her, but there was a message in there somewhere. She searched her memory for a similar conversation. Anything about options that would give her a clue where he was trying to take her.

"Yes." She agreed with his comment but tried to let her confusion show. Maybe he'd read it and drop another hint.

"Stop moving." Patricia settled in the middle of the hallway.

By Maura's measure they weren't close enough to either wall to whack Patricia's head into it. Maura could adapt. Instead of sideways, they'd go back. She'd been in enough self-defense classes to pick up some pointers. Tramp down on the instep. Heel to the knee. Go limp and drop. She knew them all.

She just had to push and then slide out of the way of the knife. Whatever it took to get her there she would do.

"You said it yourself, you need her alive." Liam continued talking in the same voice she expected he'd use to talk sports. The tone stayed even and clear. He didn't make any moves. Just walked and talked.

The mood shook Patricia. Whatever she expected from Liam clearly wasn't this. The calmer he got, the tighter she clenched her arm against Maura's throat.

"I can still mess her up pretty bad." Patricia delivered the comment like a promise.

Liam smiled then. "I have to admire you, Patricia. You have a contingency."

"I didn't have a choice after you killed Smithfield."

"You aren't the only one who walked in here with a couple of thoughts on how to get out again. I brought several weapons, thought about all of the exits and came up with strategies to get Maura out in case I couldn't do it."

Those sentences were meant for her. Maura analyzed every word Liam said, searching for the right answer. Something tickled at the edge of her mind but she couldn't grab it. Usually her brain wouldn't click off. Now she couldn't get it to turn on.

But she could make her move.

Even without heels she could make this hurt. In one swift move she rammed her butt into Patricia's stomach while stomping down on her heel as hard as possible. The move pitched their joined bodies forward and off balance. Most of Patricia's weight fell against Maura's back. The knife dangled loose in Patricia's hand, waving right in front of Maura's eyes.

Patricia's grip finally broke when Maura hurled her body in the opposite direction and threw the other woman off her. Right before she smashed into the wall, a strange tingling sensation warmed Maura's arm.

She saw the men rush forward, heard Liam's shouts mix with a woman's high-pitched squeal. Warm hands caressed her face but she could see Patricia hit the ground.

The woman landed on her back with her hands high above her head. Before she could lift the knife and launch a new line of attack, a black shoe tramped down on her wrist. She screamed as her fingers opened.

Through hazy vision, Maura dragged her gaze upward and saw Detective Spanner standing there with his gun aimed at Patricia's curled form. Maura's mind faded around the edges but she realized Spanner's presence had something to do with Liam's clues.

"Looks like I'm a bit late." Spanner smiled at her. "Dr. Lindsey, you are a woman who can take care of herself."

"Damn right." Liam leaned down to lift her off the floor.

The minute his fingers closed over her forearm, she gasped. When he pulled his hand back, his palm was stained red. "Maura?"

Horror darkened his face. Those green eyes turned cold and venomous as he glanced over at Patricia. Her rantings hadn't stopped. She swore about her husband's weakness and her ruined plans.

Maura worried Liam would kill the other woman. To settle him down and keep him with her, she brushed her hand over his cheek. "It's okay."

The combination of the touch and her words brought him back to her. "You're bleeding."

"I think she got me, but it's minor."

Dan pushed his way in. "Are you sure?"

The tingling turned to numbness as all three men crowded around her. She saw their concerned faces and refused to faint. She wanted to but drew in big gulps of air and rested her head against the wall to keep her body upright.

"I just need a minute." When her eyes eased shut, she forced them back open again.

Liam pushed Dan back as if he had the right to take over. "Here, let me see."

A hiss of pain escaped her lips as he slipped her sleeve up with gentle fingers. Any pressure sent her nerves spinning. "I probably need a bandage."

"You need an ambulance."

Spanner nodded as he clicked his radio. "Sixth-floor landing. Send a medic and officers. Come in cold."

Liam ripped the edge of his T-shirt and wrapped it around her arm. "You got my text message."

While Liam worked on Maura, Spanner took care of Patricia. He dragged her to a seated position and handcuffed her. "Don't be too happy about it. About a hundred police officers are going to storm through that door in a second."

"What did you do?" Dan asked.

The detective actually blushed. "It takes a lot to get the kind of backup I thought I needed."

Maura listened to the conversation. It happened around her and in a way that was disconnected from her, almost as if she were watching it on television. She heard the voices and saw the men hustle around. Except for a burst of pain now and then, she didn't feel anything.

A weight she couldn't identify forced her

eyes shut. Her brain fogged over as her arm began to thump. But she couldn't fall asleep. There was something important she needed to say. A point she needed Liam to understand. She had to say it before it drifted back out of her head.

She grabbed Liam's hand and pulled him in close to her. "Thank you for saving me."

He kept wrapping her arm in white material, playing nurse rather than boyfriend. "You saved yourself."

"Liam." The dryness of her voice caused it to crack.

He looked up then. "Are you in pain?"

She tried to shake her head but the headache bouncing around in there kept her from moving. "Remember that question I asked you?"

He frowned at her. "When?"

"When I was fifteen."

He spared a brief glance at Dan then gathered in even closer with his voice pitched low. "Maura, none of that matters now."

"It does because the offer still stands." She said it. The words hung out there and he could take them however he wanted.

He froze with his hands in the air and white

cotton wrapped around one of his palms. "What did you say?"

She mustered up a second reserve of energy and tried to be clearer this time. "I want you to be the one."

"You're…" Liam didn't finish the sentence. He snapped his mouth shut instead.

Spanner turned away with his hand over his mouth.

Dan cleared his throat. "What is she talking about?"

Liam still didn't move.

She worried in her slurred words and hazy state that he didn't understand her. The words that once haunted her now came easy. "You're the right man, always were."

Then she passed out.

Chapter Eighteen

Liam paced the space outside Maura's bed-room. She had refused to stay in the hospital for more than a routine checkup and some stitches. She insisted on getting home to her bed. That meant sending men ahead of them to clean up and make the place livable after the break-in.

Rather than fight her, he played along. Once Maura made up her mind, all the intelligence and common sense in the world couldn't convince her. He told her to do one thing and she immediately did the opposite.

He tried to work up a sense of frustration for the habit, but her actions just made him smile. The awkward girl had grown into a confident woman.

"How is she doing?" Detective Spanner nodded a welcome to the two police officers stationed at her front door. "Was it just the one cut?"

"The doctor is looking her over one more time, but the wound didn't go too deep. She lost some blood, but that's about it."

"She seemed ticked off in the hospital."

"Apparently, doctors do make the worst patients."

Spanner laughed. When the amusement left his face the turn was abrupt. "Patricia is being examined."

Liam never wanted to hear the woman's name again. The idea of her getting off without any jail time sent his anger spiking. "You think she qualifies for insanity?"

"Only if an obsession over money can land you there."

Liam pushed Patricia out of his mind. He vowed to stay positive for Maura's sake. After all the horrible things she'd seen today, she deserved a few hours without death.

And they had a lot to talk about. He had no idea if she remembered her words as she drifted off in that hallway, but he did. He lived for them. They kept him from losing what little control he had left after Maura hit the wall with a thud.

"Thanks for making the charges go away." Appreciation didn't always come easy for Liam, but he meant this.

Spanner shrugged it off. "The prosecutor will work it all out in the morning, but the paperwork and forensics at Smithfield, combined with the conversation I overheard, made the complex scenario pretty clear."

Liam knew Spanner did more than present a case. He fought for Maura, put up his good name against the political pressure and rumors in the media to make sure she didn't get a record or spend one night in jail.

"I owe you one." Liam held out his hand in a heartfelt gesture of gratitude.

Spanner shook it. "The department gave you a raw deal. This probably doesn't erase the debt, but it's my contribution to the cause."

"It's enough." In just a few sentences and with one act of trust in the face of incredible odds, Spanner made a dent in the anger that had been building inside Liam ever since he lost his job in a public furor.

"Call on me anytime."

When Dan joined them, Spanner said his round of goodbyes. He escorted the doctor out and dragged the other officers along with him.

The resulting quiet made Liam jumpy.

Through all the activity, talking to police and medics, Liam had avoided this conversation. The one where Dan asked the tough questions.

Dan leaned against the back of the couch and crossed his arms in front of him. "Anything you want to tell me?"

"She needed help. I wasn't about to let her down."

"You let me think she was dead."

"I really thought she was."

"Uh-huh."

Panic revved up inside Liam again. Dan was his best friend. They'd stuck by each other for years. When Liam's father pushed him aside, Dan stood by Liam's side. When everyone else abandoned Liam, Dan stepped up. The invitations didn't taper off. When he said he believed Liam acted with honor, Dan meant it.

The idea of losing Dan as a friend made Liam sick.

Liam blew out a long breath. "Look, I know I need to explain."

"Just tell me if you love her."

He didn't expect the interruption. He had his whole speech planned. All the promises about appreciating her, how he would keep her safe and take care of her forever, regardless of what else life threw them.

Dan exhaled. "It's a simple question, Liam."

"Not really."

"What I saw in that building and what I heard—I want to know what it means to you."

Dan was asking about intentions. Liam stared at the floor and fought off a laugh. "I think I should talk with Maura about that first."

"I think you should look at me."

The anger in Dan's voice grabbed Liam's attention. He raised his head and watched as Dan tightened his hands on the edge of the couch.

"You owe me honesty on this. She is my sister."

"She's also a woman."

Dan winced but didn't back down. "Then answer me."

Liam knew his friend misunderstood his

earlier reaction. This one was easy. From the time he tackled her on the deck and realized he had a second chance, he knew. They'd been circling each other for years, each maturing and learning. Without knowing it, they grew together. Their values matched. Their weaknesses and strengths complemented each other.

And the attraction raged. He ached with the need to touch her, burned with a desire to open up this last part of their relationship.

Loving Maura was the easy part.

"Yes," he said. "I love her."

The tension seeped out of the room like a balloon losing its air. Dan's shoulders even fell in what looked like relief. Liam expected the truth to set off an argument. Instead, it satisfied Dan, or seemed to.

Since Liam wasn't sure his points got through, he tried again. "She's more than a smart woman in a lab. She has so much to offer and I want to be there when she realizes it. I want to be the man who experiences the full her."

Dan nodded. "Okay."

"I'm not going to hurt her."

This time Dan raised his hand. "I said okay. I don't need the details."

"Meaning?"

Dan's mouth broke into a grin. "Call me when you're engaged."

The comment didn't rattle Liam. The idea of waking up to her, having children and planning a life appealed to him. From that, Liam knew he was in love.

Dan pushed off from the couch and started toward the door.

Liam called after him. "Where are you going?"

"Home, and I better hear from you this week."

MAURA HEARD THE FRONT DOOR CLOSE. She waited for what felt like hours for Liam's face to appear in her room. Anxiety and hope spun around in her stomach. She had no idea how he'd react to her admission.

The man just saved her life and she hit him with her virginity. Talk about putting pressure on a guy.

She knew he found her attractive. The kisses told her that much. Being serious, taking her to bed, those were separate things. He might want to walk away. She sure couldn't blame him. Fires and chases and gun battles. What man would want to join her after that sort of welcome into a relationship?

The more she sat there, the worse her nerves jumbled. She worked her mind into a confused frenzy. If he didn't come in here soon she'd…

"Feeling better?" He slipped in the doorway and didn't stop walking until he got to her bed.

"It wasn't a big deal."

"Don't kid yourself. That woman was nuts."

Maura shook her head. "I don't want to talk about Patricia Hammer or Langdon Hammer or anything to do with Smithfield Enterprises. I might never step foot in an office building again thanks to that group."

"Can't say I disagree." Liam slid his thigh on to the edge of her bed. The dip in the mattress rolled her closer to him. "What do you want to talk about?"

Men. He was going to force her to ask again.

"Forget that. I'll start." He put a hand behind her against the headboard. The other one landed on her blanket gathered on her lap. "I love you."

She felt her eyes bug out. "What?"

"Everything. All parts. The brain." He touched a finger to her forehead.

"The heart." That finger skimmed down her chest, over her breasts.

"And definitely everything in between."

She wanted to believe, but everything in her life had been so upside down lately. "This isn't some sort of delayed reaction to the violence, is it?"

He smiled. "No."

"You said that kind of fast."

"It's about falling for you." He brushed her hair back over her shoulder in a gesture laced with intimacy. "So strong and sexy. Tough and determined. I can't think of a hotter combination in a woman."

The steamy heat behind his words kicked up. "I love you, too."

His smile beamed with satisfaction. "Good."

She rushed to explain just in case they got dragged into the past and couldn't find their way out again. "This isn't the same as before. This isn't about wanting to be rescued or carried away from a life I don't understand. I can earn my own money and find my own jobs, although I clearly need a better system for picking bosses."

"Okay."

The softness around Liam's eyes gave her the motivation she needed to keep going. "I'm not a teenager."

He trailed his finger down her chest and dipped it low into deep vee between her breasts. "Oh, I can see that."

She swallowed back the rest of her explanation and jumped ahead to the part that mattered the most right that second. "I asked you a question earlier."

"You've actually asked me twice."

She gnawed on her lip. "Did you understand what I was saying?"

His thumb rubbed the raw spot she just nibbled on. "What I don't get is how someone as stunningly beautiful as you, with so much to offer a man, hasn't experienced lovemaking."

His voice didn't carry any judgment. She sensed curiosity and a touch of excitement.

"I was the wrong age at the wrong time. Then I had my work."

"You deserve every part of life, and you've been missing a good one."

"I only want you."

He brushed his fingers over the tips of her breasts. "When you're feeling better—"

"Now." The teasing and coaxing set her blood on fire. She shifted her legs and tightened her muscles to ease the tension stealing over her body.

"You're hurt."

"I want my life to start now." She wrapped her arms around his neck. She didn't want to give him a chance to back away or talk common sense. Not now.

Their mouths met in a long, lingering kiss. Energy pulsed between them as their lips traveled across each other. The churning started deep in her belly and begged for release. "I've waited long enough for you to come to me," she whispered.

He fell over her. His chest pressed her against the bed, easing her down until her back touched the mattress. "You do understand that this will change everything."

"I've read books." She tilted her head to give his mouth better access to her neck.

His eyebrow lifted along with his head. "Interesting."

"I mean I know the first time won't be perfect."

He placed a finger over her lips. "You're not being graded, but what I need you to understand is there's no going back."

Every part of her agreed. "For either of us."

"I want it all. I'm not in this for sex or an easy score. We're talking about a future and children and anything else we can build together."

When he continued to look serious, she licked her tongue around his finger. "Who knew a security guy could be so romantic?"

His other hand slipped down her body, pushing her nightgown aside and coming in contact with bare skin. "No underwear?"

"Do I need it?"

"Never."

That was the last word either of them spoke. Between kisses and touches, they learned each other's bodies. Their hands toured, brushing over skin and caressing until their nerve endings screamed for more.

When he finally came into her, the pinch

of pain took her by surprise. He kissed away the tear on her cheek and gave her time to adjust. Then she felt only pleasure. Full and complete, she grabbed on to the mattress and let the waves of pleasure course through her.

A half hour later, lying there in the dark with her arm balanced over his broad chest, she smiled.

"What has you so happy?" he asked in a sleepy, satisfied voice.

"Do you have to ask?"

He pulled back and looked down at her. "Have I thanked you for hiding out at my house?"

"You like a woman who brings trouble to your doorstep, do you?"

"I love you." He kissed the top of her head. "Everything about you."

"While we're being grateful, have I thanked you for turning me down all those years ago?"

He frowned. "I was just thinking how dumb I was to say no."

She stretched up on her elbow. "I wouldn't change anything about that time."

"You're kidding."

"We had to live those lives to earn this one."

She traced his mouth. "This is the one that matters. The one we build together."

"I always said you were smart."

"I was thinking the same thing about you."

His palm landed against her lower back. "Then you should know that anytime you want to ask the special question from now on, the answer is yes."

She laughed until he kissed her. Then she couldn't speak at all.

* * * * *

LARGER-PRINT BOOKS!

GET 2 FREE LARGER-PRINT NOVELS

HARLEQUIN®

INTRIGUE®

PLUS 2 FREE GIFTS!

Breathtaking Romantic Suspense

YES! Please send me 2 FREE LARGER-PRINT Harlequin Intrigue® novels and my 2 FREE gifts (gifts are worth about $10). After receiving them, if I don't wish to receive any more books, I can return the shipping statement marked "cancel." If I don't cancel, I will receive 6 brand-new novels every month and be billed just $4.99 per book in the U.S. or $5.74 per book in Canada. That's a saving of at least 13% off the cover price! It's quite a bargain! Shipping and handling is just 50¢ per book.* I understand that accepting the 2 free books and gifts places me under no obligation to buy anything. I can always return a shipment and cancel at any time. Even if I never buy another book from Harlequin, the two free books and gifts are mine to keep forever.

199/399 HDN E5MS

Name _____ (PLEASE PRINT) _____

Address _____ Apt. # _____

City _____ State/Prov. _____ Zip/Postal Code _____

Signature (if under 18, a parent or guardian must sign) _____

Mail to the **Harlequin Reader Service:**
IN U.S.A.: P.O. Box 1867, Buffalo, NY 14240-1867
IN CANADA: P.O. Box 609, Fort Erie, Ontario L2A 5X3
Not valid for current subscribers to Harlequin Intrigue Larger-Print books.

Are you a subscriber to Harlequin Intrigue books and want to receive the larger-print edition? Call 1-800-873-8635 today!

* Terms and prices subject to change without notice. Prices do not include applicable taxes. N.Y. residents add applicable sales tax. Canadian residents will be charged applicable provincial taxes and GST. Offer not valid in Quebec. This offer is limited to one order per household. All orders subject to approval. Credit or debit balances in a customer's account(s) may be offset by any other outstanding balance owed by or to the customer. Please allow 4 to 6 weeks for delivery. Offer available while quantities last.

Your Privacy: Harlequin Books is committed to protecting your privacy. Our Privacy Policy is available online at www.eHarlequin.com or upon request from the Reader Service. From time to time we make our lists of customers available to reputable third parties who have a product or service of interest to you. If you would prefer we not share your name and address, please check here. ☐

Help us get it right—We strive for accurate, respectful and relevant communications. To clarify or modify your communication preferences, visit us at www.ReaderService.com/consumerschoice.

HILP10R

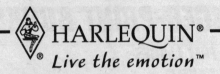

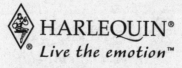

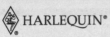

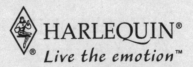

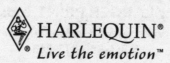

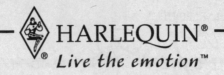

Love Inspired®
SUSPENSE
RIVETING INSPIRATIONAL ROMANCE

Watch for our new series of
edge-of-your-seat suspense novels.
These contemporary tales
of intrigue and romance
feature Christian characters
facing challenges to their faith...
and their lives!

NOW AVAILABLE IN REGULAR
& LARGER-PRINT FORMATS

Steeple
Hill®

Visit:
www.SteepleHill.com

Silhouette

SPECIAL EDITION™

Emotional, compelling stories that capture the intensity of living, loving and creating a family in today's world.

Special Edition features bestselling authors such as Susan Mallery, Sherryl Woods, Christine Rimmer, Joan Elliott Pickart— and many more!

For a romantic, complex and emotional read, choose Silhouette Special Edition.

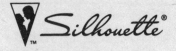